The Secret of the Sea

Donna Stevenson

www.innovativeinkpublishing.com
Send all inquiries to:
4050 Westmark Drive
Dubuque, IA 52004-1840

ISBN: 9-798-7657-4509-0

Published in the United States of America

Acknowledgements

Thank you to James Warren, author of *Troy and Toad* and *The Boy in the Box*, as well as numerous short stories; Frances Young-Bennet, author of *The Shining Place*; and John Bennet, writer of *Alfred Hitchcock, Charles Bennett, & The Rise of the Modern Mystery Thriller*. Your thoughtful and valuable suggestions over the years helped make this novel happen.

To Karen Grencik at Fox Literary, thank you for taking a chance on me.

And finally, and most especially, to Bob, whose love and encouragement helped me believe in myself. You're forever in my heart.

Contents

Chapter 1

I'm late! Throwing back the covers, I jump into my jeans, pull on a sweatshirt and a faded Angels' baseball cap, snatch up a pair of white slip-on Vans, and tip-toe past Dad's room. He's still snoring, and Izzie hasn't arrived yet. Grabbing my key off the hook in the kitchen, I ease open the door and slip out of the cottage.

It's cool and damp but clear, a perfect June morning. The sky glimmers with pale, pre-dawn light. I hurry down the hill, hopping along on one foot as I struggle into my shoes, then set off at a run, pausing only to glance both ways before darting across Pacific Coast Highway. I should jog the extra block to the traffic light on Cliff Drive, but I don't want to miss seeing Nessie, the beautiful seal. Besides, there are no cars.

Izzie would slay me if she knew.

Dashing down cement steps of the main entrance to Fisherman's Cove, I smell the sharp tang of the ocean and leap over the last three stairs. I pull off my shoes and toss them aside, breaking for the shore's edge.

She's here! Her iridescent tail shines like a prism catching the faint rays of light as she dives. I wait for her to surface again and spot me. It seems like forever, but finally, periscope-like, her head rises a few yards down, near the rocks. She turns expectantly, rising higher, her eyes boring into mine. I stand on tip-toe, waving.

"Hi Nessie!!" I yell, cupping my hands around my mouth.

Nessie's gold-brown coat glistens in the slick saltwater. I let people think I named her after the Loch Ness monster, but I'm not that stupid. Nessie is no monster. The first time I saw her, her sleek head slowly emerged from the water, and she looked straight at me, into my soul, an invisible silver thread connecting us. The word *Necessity* popped into my mind. Necessity. Nessie is my necessity.

I can't explain why. Some things just are.

She's the most dazzling, exquisite thing I've ever seen.

Nessie strains forward as if wanting to speak, then turns her head, motioning toward a spot in the sand. I sprint down the beach, not taking my eyes off her, but she does a back-flip and is gone just as I reach her spot.

"Nessie, come back! *Please!*" I plead. I peer out, my hand across my forehead to shield my eyes from the faint sun beginning to glare on the ocean, but it's no use—she's gone. Plopping down on the sand with disappointment, I cross my arms over my knees and watch the waves, taking in the sounds and smells of the ocean. At least she came, I console myself. A crab the size of my palm scuttles out of the rocks.

Crabs always remind me of my mother. We used to go crab hunting together until she ran away when I was five. I only remember her a little, her dark hair flying in the wind, tickling my face as she swung me around, pretending to toss me into the waves. I remember, though sometimes I wish I didn't.

I still hear her voice with its lilting accent, singing me to sleep with an Irish lullaby. I even remember some of the words:

> Over the mountain, over the sea,
> Back where my heart is longing to be,
> Oh, let the light that shines on me,
> Shine on the one I love.

Love. Yeah, right. She loved me so much she left me. Sometimes the anger buzzes in my head like an angry wasp.

I curl my toes in the sand, staring out at the water. Where are you, Mom? Why did you leave me? The familiar, smothering sigh escapes, the one that makes Dad's eyes wet.

I watch the crab's progress along the sand. A sudden impulse takes over, and I grab it and toss it into the ocean. Stupid crab. Who needs it, anyway? I watch as it floats out to sea, unharmed.

And that's when I see it—something written in the wet sand. I hop up to get a better look.

AURORA.

Just like that, my name marring the smooth, dark wetness of the shoreline. Each elegant letter curls like a ribbon. Startled, I scan the beach, the water, and the shadowed cliffs with homes precariously dangling from their edges, and the winding path leading behind through the neighborhood. Not a soul in sight.

Who would write *that* name in the sand? Someone must be playing a trick and a not-very-funny one! Everyone calls me Arie, even Dad.

Mom named me Aurora, and that alone is a reason to hate it. Why did she stick me with a Disney-princess name? That stupid girl sleeping her life away for a hundred years waiting for some fool of a prince to figure out how to get into the castle. She should be called Sleeping Dummy, not Sleeping Beauty. I like a good story as well as the next kid, but I'm not a sissy-baby who believes in fairies or Santa Claus or monsters under the bed. After all, I'm almost thirteen. Besides, I know there are stranger things out there—real things.

So, if it isn't Dad or Izzie, who could it be? I blink and see his name burning behind my eyelids—Billy Hernandez, the only other person who knows my secret. He wouldn't *dare*.

But it must be him. There is no one else. Not even Angelina knows, and she's been my friend since last year in fifth grade when she pushed Axel, a sixth-grade bully, in the mud for picking on a little kid.

You've got to admire a girl like that.

"I'm going to get you good for this, Billy," I mutter. Snatching off my cap, I throw it hard into the sand for emphasis. Smooth move, Arie. All that got you was a wet, sandy hat. I pick it up and turn around, expecting Billy to be hiding in the bushes, laughing.

Still alone. I kick the sand around, wiping out my name. I shake the hat and grab my shoes, taking the path through the houses. It's a private entrance, one only locals use. Most tourists never find Fisherman's Cove, tucked as it is between two high mounds of rock on each side and a hill behind filled with homes.

I practically stomp up the steep weather-worn wood steps, slapping the wet hat against my leg, contemplating what I'm going to do to Billy.

Chapter 2

What would be the best way to get back at Billy? A list begins to form in my head as I take my anger out on the pavement:

1. Start a rumor that he still wears Spiderman pajamas. Hmmm. Not mean enough.

2. Put a frog in his backpack. He hates frogs. No, that wouldn't be fair to the frog. It might get hurt.

3. Send him a fake love letter from Amanda Peters, a girl he's crushed on since fourth grade. That's it. Sneaky and mean. I like it.

Lost in plotting my revenge, I haven't noticed traffic has thickened. I better hurry or Izzie will squawk, and Dad will be cross. He doesn't like me spending time at the beach. It makes him nervous.

As I turn the corner, our snug, single story cottage glistens in the morning light. Ivy trails around the oak tree that stands guard by the house and up the sides of the walls. Everything's in bloom. Izzie and I planted irises and daffodils last October in alternating patterns along the porch, brush strokes of yellow and purple against the white. Admiring the results of our labors, I run a finger along the silky petals, soothing my boiling emotions.

"Arie! I've been worried sick. You should have been home fifteen minutes ago." Dad pushes open the screen and lumbers down the steps. He's not the smallest man that ever lived (he's six feet four inches and not exactly thin) and reminds me a little of an elephant seal, but he's a gentle giant. The teacher said that elephant seals can be mean, but I don't believe her.

"I wish you'd stay away from that ocean. It's not safe. Or at least don't go so early."

Here we go again, the same old lecture. "Sorry, Dad. But I'm okay, see?" I do a little twirl to show him. Dad always fusses about what he calls my early-bird ways but hasn't yet forbidden my dawn excursions.

He puts his arm around my shoulders, giving me a friendly shake, holding me at arm's length, pretending to inspect for damage. Then he grabs my moist, sandy hat.

"What happened to your hat? Have you been too close to the water again?" Dad frowns, emphasizing the wrinkles between his deep-hazel eyes. For the first time, I notice streaks of grey in his sand-brown hair.

"I just dropped it in the wet part on the slope," I answer, trying to be patient. Adults can be so frustrating sometimes.

"I can't stress the importance of you staying away from that water, Arie," he begins his boring rant about the ocean, "even to wade. You might get knocked over by a wave, and then what? You're not allowed . . .."

"I know, Dad, I know," I cut him off, "but I'm almost thirteen! I *can* swim, you know." Really, he worries too much. If he has his way, I'll never learn to surf. Dad would have a seizure if he knew about my secret dream. Izzie had to talk him into letting me take swimming lessons, saying it's not safe to live near the ocean and not know how to swim. It turns out I'm a natural. I've been saving up for surf lessons for over a year, running errands and doing extra chores for Izzie, stashing half my allowance from Dad, as well as last year's birthday money.

Dad leans over, knees bending slightly, his hands braced on his thighs, and looks me in the eyes. "I guess you are growing up, sweetie," he sighs, "but promise me you'll be careful, and don't try to swim in that ocean. If you want to swim, go to the community pool."

Seriously, why would I want to swim in a crowded pool? "I promise, Dad. Pinky swear." I cross my fingers on one hand behind my back, holding my pinky out, trying not to roll my eyes. Too trusting, he crooks his pinky around mine. If he knew I swim in the ocean all the time, he'd ground me for life. How can I explain that in the water, I feel super-powered and alive and at home? He'd never understand.

"Let's go in and see what Izzie has cooked up for breakfast," he says.

***

On the way to school, Dad asks, "What are you up to in class these days, sweetie?" "We read *Julie of the Wolves* and now we're tracing Julie's route on a big map of Alaska. Then we're going to the computer lab to look up all the animals and plants that are in the book."

"That sounds fun," Dad replies.

"And I get to research seals! I begged Mrs. Krenwinkle and she said yes. Most of the kids want to do wolves or bears, but not me." I quiver at the thought of spending a dreamy hour choosing pictures of seals for my report. "I'm going to be a marine biologist when I grow up."

Dad's jaw tightens as he squirms in his seat. "What's the matter, Dad? Don't you like seals?" I demand.

"I like seals just fine, sweetie, just fine," he replies, but he doesn't sound too convincing.

Though Izzie knows about Nessie, I've never told my dad. I asked Izzie to keep it a secret. Dad hasn't liked the sea since Mom left. I wish I knew why he hates the ocean so much. I asked him once, but he just waved his hand in the direction of the beach and said, "It's dangerous," and walked away.

Izzie says he used to scuba dive in Diver's Cove, but I saw him throw away all his scuba gear when he cleaned the garage three years ago. He glances at me with a pained smile as we pull to the curb in front of my school—El Morro Elementary. I feel awkward, like I've said something wrong.

"Here we are!" he says a little loud, trying too hard.

"Thanks, Dad!" I try hard back. I give him a quick peck on the cheek and grab my backpack. He's been acting funny lately, staring off into space like he's got some big secret, and he has increased his campaign to keep me out of the ocean.

"Don't forget your sweater." He reaches into the back seat and hands it to me as I'm scrambling out of the car. "I'll see you tonight."

Shutting the door, I wave, then head to the playground to find Billy. I spot him near the four-square courts, bouncing a ball under his legs and around his back. Tall and gawky, Billy towers over the other boys, and despite his nerdiness, no one bullies him.

"Billy Hernandez," I yell, pounding across the yard.

"Hey, Arie. What's up?" He stops bouncing the ball and holds it tucked under his arm.

He knows when I'm mad. It's the only time I use his last name. Usually I call him Billy-willy or silly-Billy, and sometimes idiot if he's goofing around too much. I get right up in his face, so close I can smell his peanut butter breath. One hand on my hip clutches my sweater, the other balls into a fist which I shake in his face so hard my backpack dances the Mambo.

"You promised not to tell anyone!" I practically spit it at him. "Then I find it written in the sand. You know I don't want anyone to know my real name."

He scrunches one eye and tilts his head, brows knitted. "What're you talking about, Arie? You sound nuts."

"Nuts?!" I screech. "Maybe so, but at least I can keep a secret!"

"Stop spitting on me!" he says, wiping his cheek on his shirt with a look of disgust. "Chill out. Everybody's staring." He grabs me by the arm and hauls me a few yards onto the grassy area where no one can hear. "What's wrong?"

"Don't play dumb. You're the only person who could have done it. No one else knows my real name but Dad and Izzie." I shake my arm free.

"Done what?" he asks, irritation needling his voice.

"Wrote my name in the sand at the cove, that's what!" I cross my arms and glare at him.

With that dumbfounded expression he gets when he can't puzzle something out, he says, "What? Someone wrote your name in the sand?"

"Yes, plain as day, A-U-R-O-R-A.

He shifts the ball to his other hand. "Your *full* name?! Well, *I* didn't do it! I know how much you hate it."

His intense brown eyes tell the truth. Billy and I have been best friends since kindergarten. If I hadn't been so angry, I would have known Billy wasn't the culprit.

"If you didn't, who did?" I ask, slightly subdued.

"I don't know, but if I find out, I'll sock 'em one for you." He grins like a moron.

"Oh, like that will help," I reply, dripping sarcasm. "But Izzie wouldn't play a rotten trick like that, and Dad never goes to the beach anymore." We stand quiet, thinking.

Frowning, Billy finally says. "Maybe some guy with a crush found out your name and wrote it."

"Don't be silly. How would some other kid find out my name?"

The bell rings and we head to class.

Angelina, Billy, and I sit next to each other in the computer lab. Billy searches for golden plovers, and Angelina is working on wolves. I flip through pictures of seals but find none that can match Nessie. I print a few pages of seal facts and email some pictures to print at home in color. Then I find a video of seals and put on the headphones.

Sleek bodies glide in and out of the water, and their mournful cries and moans make me sad, like a lost refrain of a song, so unlike the harsh barks of the sea lions. I feel funny all over but don't want to stop watching their fluent moves or listening to their eerie, lovely voices—even if they do make me want to cry. Mesmerized, I don't hear Mrs. Krenwinkle announce "Time's up" like she always does. Billy pinches my arm, jolting me out of my daydream, nodding toward our teacher. Reluctantly, I turn off the video and remove the headphones. We gather up our research and walk back to our classroom.

Billy leans over and whispers, "Let's make a plan to catch the mystery writer. Meet me after school and we'll explore the cove. Should we invite Angelina?"

"Okay," I whisper back, remembering she wants to be a detective. Maybe she can help find out who is targeting me and why. "But I don't want to tell her my real name."

Billy tilts his head and gives me his *Whatever* face of exasperation.

Chapter 3

After school, we catch up with Angelina.

"Hey, Angelina, do you want to come with us to the cove?" I ask.

One side of her lip curves upward into an almost-smile. "Why? What for?"

"Just to hang out and watch for seals. We might need your detective skills to solve a mystery." Billy kicks a rock into the air, almost hitting a kid in the head.

Angelina's dark blue eyes look from me to Billy and back to me. She nods. "Why not? I ain't doin' nothing' else."

"Do you need to call your mom to let her know where you're going? You can use my cell phone," I offer, knowing she doesn't have one.

"No, but thanks. My mom doesn't get home until about 7:00, so as long as I'm home by then, it's okay." She tosses her head in that defiant way she always uses to say she doesn't want anyone feeling sorry for her. "So, what's this big mystery?"

Billy looks at me with a question in his eyes. I give a reluctant nod and answer, "Someone wrote my name in the sand."

"We're trying to catch whoever did it," Billy butts in. "We figure you've been reading all those detective stories, you might be able to help."

"Somebody has been writing *Arie* in the sand? That's weird," she says. "Any idea who?"

"No idea. And what's *really* weird is no one knows my real name but Billy," I say. "I'll have to tell you if you're going to help, but you have to promise not to tell anyone, especially at school. I'd die of embarrassment."

"That bad, huh?" she smirks. "Okay, I promise."

Flatly, I state, "It's Aurora."

Angelina tries to stifle a laugh, and it comes out a little strangled. "Like the Disney princess? You hate all those princesses!"

"Yeah, that's the one," Billy answers. Then he gets infected and snorts his unique brand of guffawing.

"Stop laughing! It's not funny," I cross my arms against my chest and scowl.

Then I find myself laughing with them. By the time we stop, we've reached Fisherman's Cove.

"Is that seal still coming around? What was it you called her?" Angelina asks.

"Yes, her name is Nessie. She's the most beautiful seal in the world," I say, perhaps with too much passion.

"So, you've seen all the seals in the world, huh?" she says, looking amused.

I stick out my tongue at her.

"Where is she?" Angelina scans the ocean.

"It's too crowded. She won't come tonight," I say. "Come with us when it's not so busy."

"Cool," she says.

The fog has rolled in, bringing a chill with its dampness. We toss our backpacks by the path and sleuth the sand from one end of the beach to the other. Nothing.

"Show me where your name was written," Billy says, all business-like.

"Okay, Sherlock Holmes," I laugh but Billy pretends not to notice my brilliant wit. Angelina, Billy, and I both spent last summer at the library reading stories for the Sherlock Holmes read-a-thon. The one who read the most stories won a gift certificate to Laguna Beach Books. Angelina won. "Right there!" I point to the offensive spot.

"Hmmm," Billy mutters, rubbing his chin as if in deep thought, studying the sand.

He really cracks me up sometimes, but I know he wants to help, so I choke back my smart-aleck remarks.

Angelina gets down on her knees and inspects the area. It does look like *something* has been written there, maybe an 'R.' It's hard to tell." She stands and brushes the sand off her knees.

Another wave washes in, wiping away the last curls of my name.

"Let's climb the rocks and see if we find anything in Shaw's Cove," he suggests.

"Sure, why not?" Billy might be onto something. "It won't hurt to look."

We make our way over the rocks and down the other side. When the tide comes in, it swallows these rocks, and we have to walk all the way around on the street. Shaw's is a longer beach, much tidier than Fisherman's Cove with its stacks of worn kayaks and paint-peeled boats shoved into the rocks out of the tide's way. The sturdy homes in Shaw's Cove have more class, with their large, pristine white houses, gleaming picture windows, and tall iron gates to keep out the riff-raff, like Billy and me, I suppose.

NO TRESSPASSING signs mar the otherwise perfect community. I prefer the houses in Fisherman's, piled haphazardly on one other, a little worn but friendlier with their grubby, small windows and collections of shells decorating the railings and stairs. People lounge on their porches, sipping drinks, laughing and talking, and will give a friendly wave to a kid. Not here. Too straight-backed and somber, these homes, and I've never once seen anyone use the perfect balconies.

One day, I saw a maid in a uniform watering the airy green ferns and neatly trimmed red azalea shrubs growing majestically out of their pots. One rabble-rouser had the nerve to slip a blossom out through the wrought-iron railing. She took out a pair of scissors and cut off its head. It made me think of poor Marie Antoinette we learned about in history.

As we stroll down the beach, Billy abruptly halts, digging his heels into the sand, and grabs my arm.

"Look!" He points down the beach.

At first, I can't find what's he's pointing at, but then I see a kid with a stick, writing in the sand. "He looks kinda little," I say, doubtfully.

"Come on! Let's find out what he's writing," Billy urges, ignoring my protests.

"Okay, Billy-Willie, but let go of my arm. You're giving me a bruise."

He lets go like a snake bit him. "Sorry," he mumbles.

"Maybe the kid has a crush on you," Angelina offers. "Little kids get crushes all the time."

"I've never seen him before. How would he know my name?"

Angelina shrugs. We walk along, all casual-like so the kid doesn't notice us. He's a small squirt, about eight years old, intent on his task. He's in the wet part of the sand, and we stand on the dry slope behind him, trying to make out what he's writing.

"I can't tell, can you?" I whisper.

"No, but I'm gonna find out." Billy takes two long strides down the slope and looms over the boy, who looks up, startled.

"What ya writin,' kid?" Billy gives a good performance as an ax murderer. The boy's bright blue eyes widen, and he drops the stick.

"N-nothing," he stammers.

"Let's see," Billy neatly side-steps him, peering squinty-eyed at the sand.

"Hey, that's none of your business!" The boy balls up a fist in defiance.

I have to hand it to him. He's got guts standing up to Billy, who's not only twice his size but about five years older. I could have told him Billy's a big bluffer, a softie who would never hurt a flea much less a small boy.

"Don't get your skivvies in a twist, kid. I'm just curious," Billy says, gentle-like, probably realizing he has scared the boy. Angelina and I move closer, trying to make out the crooked words. We look at each other and smile. I LOVE REESE" is carved into the sand, the 'O" shaped like a heart.

"Having love problems, kid?" Billy asks.

"Yeah," he says, staring at his feet, "but she likes someone else."

In sync, Billy and I sit down, crossed-legged, with Angelina following. The boy deflates like a balloon, sliding onto the damp sand in front of us.

"What's your name?" Billy asks.

"Trevor," he mumbles.

"Well, Trevor, have you told Reese you like her?"

Trevor turns his baby-blues on Billy. "Should I? What if she laughs at me?"

His anxious little freckled-from-the-sun face makes me want to laugh and cry. He's going to be a heartbreaker in the not-so-far-off future.

"Well, I wouldn't march up to her and blurt it out. Girls like to be wooed. Start off by giving her a little present, like a shell, nothing fancy. See how she reacts. Keep your eyes on her face; you'll be able to tell," Billy advises.

I turn my head to stare at Billy. He's full of surprises. Trevor's face glows like a firefly.

Angelina is biting her lip, trying not to smile.

"What's wooed mean?" he asks, drawing out the "o's" like an owl, his face scrunched in puzzlement.

"It means you have to do nice things for a girl if you want her attention," I reply before Billy says something dumb.

"Will that work?" Trevor asks, hope in his throat.

"It's worth a try. Why don't you give it a try tomorrow, then we'll meet you here after school, same time, okay? You can tell us how it went."

Trevor gazes at Billy like he's Captain America.

"What's *your* names?" Trevor asks, gouging a trough in the sand with his toe.

"I'm Billy and this is Arie and Angelina. So, Trevor, do you live in this cove?" Billy questions.

"I live right there, in that house." He points to the Marie Antoinette estate.

"Wow, that's a nice place," Angelina says, giving it an appreciative gaze.

"Looks like you've got a nice view from there." Billy thoughtfully studies the house.

"Yep. I can see parts of Crystal Cove and Fisherman's from the balcony, sometimes, if there's no fog," Trevor brags, "especially with my telescope."

"You have a telescope?" Billy and I ask at the same time. We exchange looks.

"Being wealthy sure has its perks," Angelina says, a little envy edging her voice.

Trevor vigorously nods his head, "Dad bought it for me for Christmas last year. We keep it on the balcony to watch the stars. I'm going to be an astronomer when I grow up."

"That's great," Billy nods. Do me a favor, sport. If you see anything suspicious, like someone writing in the sand in Fisherman's Cove, or someone hanging around there that looks like they don't belong, let me know, okay?"

"Okay, but why?"

"We're trying to solve a mystery, and you can help."

"What mystery?" Trevor practically quivers with excitement.

"It's a secret, squirt. We can't tell you yet," Billy replies.

"Oh," Trevor says, disappointed. "Okay, I'll be the lookout. I'll check every day."

"That would be a big help," I tell him.

"We need to get over the rocks before the tide comes in." Billy ruffles his head like Izzie does mine.

As we rise to shake the sand from our jeans, Trevor pops up like a buoy.

"Okay, thanks!" Trevor sticks out his hand for a shake, all smiles. Billy takes it and gives it a man-like pump. Trevor repeats the ceremony with me.

Angelina gives him a fist bump instead and says, "Don't worry, kid. Those killer eyes of yours are bound to win her over."

We head down the beach. Finally, I say to Billy, "Look at you, giving advice to the lovelorn. When did you get so wise?"

"I've picked up a thing or two here and there," he replies, like it's no big deal.

Angelina snorts.

"You don't fool me, Silly-Billy," I tease. "You've got a crush on some girl and have been studying up. Who is she? Amanda *Peters*?"

"Nobody you'd know," he teases back. "For your information, I stopped liking Amanda last year. Why, are you *jealous*?" He thrusts his shoulder into me, making me stumble.

I laugh and shove him with the palm of my hand. "In your dreams!"

"You had a crush on *Amanda Peters*?" Angelina hoots. "She's such a girlie-girl. I didn't think she'd be your type."

"She's not," Billy says, sounding annoyed. "It was just a kid crush.

"Oh, *sure*," she says.

The advancing tide has pitched a few stray waves over the rocks, making them slippery, but we make it over just in time.

We retrieve our backpacks at the mouth of the path and start the climb.

"I'm sorry we didn't find anything," Billy says, serious now. "Why don't we try in the morning before school? We might have a better chance then."

"I can't come in the morning. Mom always insists on dropping me off at school, saying she wants to spend more time with me. I guess she thinks I'll turn into a juvenile delinquent or something," Angelina says, with more than a bit of sarcasm.

"But she lets you walk home? That doesn't make sense," Billy says.

"Yeah, tell me about it," she responds. "Parents." She shakes her head.

Billy and I nod in agreement.

After Angelina turns off at PCH to go home, I say to Billy, "Okay. I'll meet you at the cove at 5:30 before the sun comes all the way up."

"How about I meet you in front of your house and we can go together?"

"Good idea. Then you can come back to my house for breakfast. We can go to school from there. I'll ask Izzie and text you later."

"Ask her if she'll make waffles," Billy enthusiastically replies.

Izzie's waffles are legendary. She's the best baker in Laguna Beach.

We say our goodbyes at the top of the hill.

"IZZIE!" I shout as I bang through the door, tossing my backpack on a nearby chair.

"I'm not deaf, child, at least not yet," she walks out of the compact kitchen, drying her hands on her bright yellow apron that states 'Kiss the Cook,' "but I will be if you keep making so much noise."

"Sorry, Izzie," I apologize, but she knows I'm not at all sorry, so she gathers me in a big hug, squeezing like a giant anaconda, until I grunt in protest. Then she abruptly let's go. She's a short woman, only a couple of inches taller than me, stern and scolding, soft and plump, and I know she loves me. Her eyes light up when she sees me, even when she's miffed. Though her hugs crush me to the bone, I love her back.

"So, what has you so fired up you come crashing through the door like a rhino, yelling like the house is burning down?" She ruffles my short, boyish, caramel-colored hair until it stands up, porcupine-like, but I don't mind. It's our ritual. It wouldn't feel like home without Izzie messing up my hair.

"Billy's coming with me to the cove tomorrow morning. Can he come back with me for breakfast?"

"Sure thing, Sugar Plum," she replies. "Just make sure he asks his mom first. That boy sure can eat. I think his stomach is in the bottom of his feet," Izzie says in her pleased-as-punch voice. "What would you like for breakfast?"

"Waffles or pancakes."

"You just had waffles this morning! You're going to turn into one if you keep that up," she remarks.

"*Izzie,* that trick hasn't worked since I was five!"

"I'll make pancakes with lots of toppings to choose from, but you'll need to eat some fruit and protein to compete with all that sugar."

"Thanks, Izzie, you're the best!"

"And don't you forget it, Sugar Plum," she warns.

Chapter 4

I bounce out of bed at 5:20, just before my purple, fuzzy-cat alarm meows. Glancing at that clock always reminds me why I can't have a real kitten. Dad's allergic. I should throw the clock out—it's missing chunks of fur and one plastic eye dangles by a thread, giving it a slightly demented look—but somehow can't bear to. I've had it as long as I can remember.

"Izzie, have you seen my notebook?" I yell, as I cram things into my backpack for school.

"I think I saw it on the table in the hall," she yells back. "And I am not your personal tracking device," she adds with a loud humph.

It's there, under a pile of mail. As I shove aside the advertisements and bills, I notice a handwritten postcard. Who sends postcards these days? Curious, I pick it up and study the picture. It looks like a mansion, complete with towers and manicured lawns. I turn it over. University of Indiana is typed in the left hand corner. In small loopy writing it says,

> Dear Jerry,
>
> Though it may seem old-fashioned to send a postcard, I wanted a more personal expression of what a nice time I've had these past few months. I'm excited about seeing you in July and meeting Arie. She sounds charming.
>
> Always,
> M.

Who's M? Dad hasn't mentioned getting to know anyone. He has taken a lot of business trips to conferences, more than usual, now that I think about it. And he's acting weird, more distracted and goofier, smiling to himself like he has discovered another King Tut. Could it be a girl? The note sure sounds like a girl wrote it. No, Dad never dates. It must be a new friend who teaches cultural anthropology like Dad. Maybe a female friend. They probably sit around talking about boring stuff like the social habits of a lost tribe in the Amazon. I toss it into the pile and shove my notebook into my backpack.

Billy's waiting for me, sitting on the porch steps, his backpack already stashed behind the red floral wicker chair. We decide to jog because we hope to make the track team next year in junior high, so we train every chance we get. Billy also wants to be a lifeguard when he's old enough, and he's planning to take surfing lessons with me, even though he's been surfing for years with his dad. Another month and summer will be here. I can't wait!

Playing it safe, we cross at the light, then sneak down the path past the houses so we can surprise the mystery writer. We hide behind the rocks and watch for a while but no luck.

"Nuts to this," Billy complains, "let's check it out."

Kicking off our shoes, we race across the sand, halting at the water's edge.

At first, I don't see anything, but then I can make out some faint letters, faded by the ins and outs of the gentle morning tide. "Look!"

"I don't see anything," he says.

"It's right there," I yell, pointing.

Then he sees it, a little way down the beach, written in the same spot as before. *Aurora.*

Startled, Billy takes a step back. "And I thought you made up the story because you wanted to spend more time with me," he jokes.

In response, I give him my usual punch in the arm. "Don't flatter yourself. Get serious." We scan the beach. No one. As we get closer to the spot, I see something shining at the end of my name in the early morning rays, like a gleaming period. Billy picks it up and hands it to me without a word.

It's a tiny shell with a pea-size, creamy-pink and blue roundish stone nesting inside.

I delicately lift it out of its resting place, rolling it between my thumb and forefinger, its silky texture cool to the touch. Puzzled, I look up at Billy's serious face.

"The mystery deepens," he says, for lack of anything else, I guess.

"Who could be doing this?" I ask in a hushed tone. Something tugs at my memory, but I can't quite shake it out.

"Beats me. Let me see it." I hand the stone and shell to Billy, who carefully inspects both. "This looks like an abalone pearl, the rarest on earth. My dad won't believe this!" Billy's dad's a jeweler, and Billy likes to help out in the shop, so he'd know.

Billy shakes his head. "I don't know what to think, Arie." He hands back the treasures, and I zip them into the pocket of my board shorts.

We make our regular search of the beach and rocks and head back to the house.

"Don't say anything to Izzie or my dad about the pearl," I tell Billy, "or your dad."

"Why not?" he asks.

"I don't know. I have a funny feeling maybe I shouldn't tell anyone else—at least not yet." I'm mystified and a little bit worried. It's getting weirder.

"What about Angelina?" he asks.

"We have to tell her, Silly-Billy, so she can help."

It's such a perfect morning with the sun already warm on our faces, making Billy's already tanned skin shine; my grey mood evaporates like the fog. His deep brown eyes, flecked with gold, are almost as beautiful as Nessie's. We wade in the gentle waves and search for sea glass. Billy finds a rare blue piece, pounded smooth, and gives it to me.

"Thanks, Billy," I say, feeling suddenly awkward. Usually, we fight over the blue pieces. It's unlike Billy to surrender such a prize. "Are you sure?"

"Yeah, I've got plenty because I'm better at hunting than you are," he says.

I give him the eye roll, and we're back to normal. I put Billy's gift in with shell and pearl.

"I'm hungry," he complains, "let's go."

* * *

At school, it's hard to focus. I sit at my desk, lost in thought, fingering the pearl in my pocket.

"Arie McGinnis!" I hear the sharp sound of Mrs. Krenwinkle when she's irritated. "Pay attention!"

"Sorry," I mumble.

"I asked if you have an outline for your report."

"Oh. No. I'm sorry. I've been busy." What a lame excuse. Her narrow eyes tell me she doesn't buy it either.

"If you don't have it by tomorrow, you'll be docked points."

"Okay," I mutter. I try harder to pay attention, but I don't have much luck.

After school, the three of us head back to Shaw's Cove to keep our promise to Trevor, deciding to skip Fisherman's because the tide is high. If anyone wrote anything else in the sand, it would be washed away by now. We fill Angelina in on the pearl.

"That's creepy!" Angelina says, her eyebrows knitted with alarm. "You better tell your dad."

"No way." I shake my head. "Huh-uh. He'll never let me leave the house again. Why, are you *scared?*"

"I am *not.*" Her mouth is tight and she shoots me the stink-eye.

Trevor's there, waiting for us.

"Hi!" he shouts, as he runs, arms pumping, to meet us.

"Hey, sport," Billy greets him, "how'd it go with Reese?"

"Yeah, tell us what happened, and don't leave anything out," I tell Trevor. "We want all of the details." In unison, we sit, forming a circle. Trevor, excitement oozing from every pore, begins his story.

"I did like you said, Billy. I gave her half of a purple geode I found hiking with my dad. I waited until she was alone on the playground."

"What did she say?" I prompt.

"She said it was the nicest present anyone ever gave her!"

His triumphant expression amuses me.

"Atta boy, give me a high five," Billy raises his hand for Trevor to smack.

Trevor resembles a balloon about to burst.

Trevor chatters on for a while, and then says, "I almost forgot! I saw someone on the rocks last night."

"Way to bury the lead," Billy mutters, but smiles patiently. "What'd you see, kid?"

"I saw a lady on the rocks by Fisherman's Cove where waves were crashing. It's dangerous, my mom says, to enter the water from the rocks. I yelled but don't think she heard me. When I looked through my telescope, she was gone. All I saw was a black blob, like a coat or something."

"Hmmmm." Billy glances from Trevor to the rocks. "Your eyes must be playing tricks on you."

"Maybe," Trevor replies. "But it sure looked like a lady."

"Thanks, Trevor," I brush a lock of sandy hair out of his eyes. "We really appreciate your help."

"Yeah, good spying," Billy compliments him, and Trevor's grin almost cracks his face in half.

We say goodbye, leaving Trevor to finish carving hearts in the sand. As we walk up the hill, Billy says, "Who do you think that lady could be?"

"How should I know? It's probably just some woman who likes to walk on the beach at night." For a second, I wonder if it could be my mom. I bat the thought away like I'm shooing away a bothersome gnat.

Chapter 5

The next morning, I hear Dad bumbling around in the kitchen. He usually sleeps at least an hour longer than I do because he stays up late, working, either grading papers or preparing lectures.

"Hi Dad. You're up early."

"Hello, sweetheart," he says, smiling that goofy smile he's been wearing lately, reminding me about the mysterious postcard from Indiana. "I have an early breakfast meeting."

"Oh. Is it someone from Indiana?" I ask, catching him by surprise.

Running his hand through his hair in that nervous gesture I know so well, he stammers, "What makes you ask that?"

"I saw the postcard in the hallway. Who's 'M'?"

"Have you been going through my mail?" His voice has a hard edge to it I've never heard before.

"No," I say, indignant and dismayed that he would talk to me like that. "I haven't been going through your *mail*. It was on top of my notebook." I glare at him. Since when does he keep secret mail?

He shoots daggers at me, then says, "It's a friend."

"What kind of friend?" I put one hand on my hip and stare him down.

His eyes drop from mine and his voice goes into neutral as he pretends to brush invisible lint off of his tie. "It's just a friend I met at a conference."

"Why is he coming here?"

Dad's eyes shift sideways, avoiding mine. What is he up to?

"To visit, Miss Nosy Britches," he answers, his tone more friendly now. "I need to go or I'll be late." He kisses the top of my head, grabs his briefcase, and heads out the door so fast, you'd think he was meeting with the Queen of England instead of a bunch of stuffy old professors.

After school, the three of us check both coves—no mysterious gifts and no Trevor.

"Hey, maybe Homeless Harry knows who the mystery writer is," Billy says, sounding like he just discovered a new planet. "Or maybe he's the mystery writer."

Everyone in Laguna Beach knows Harry. He's been living on the beach for years. "I doubt Harry even knows my name," I say, "but it's a good idea. He might have seen something." I hadn't thought about Harry in a long time. "I'll ask Izzie about him. I think she takes him food sometimes."

"Are you going back tonight to watch for Nessie?"

"Of course," I scoff. "You know I always do."

"I better come with you. Something strange is going on. Maybe you shouldn't go there alone anymore."

"I've been going there by myself for two years. I'm not going to stop now just because someone's playing a stupid trick," I reply.

"Just let me go with you, Arie, okay. At least until we solve this mystery."

"Aye aye, Captain," I stop and salute him. He lightly whacks me in the arm.

"Ouch!!" I holler, joking "That's gonna bruise!"

"Serves you right!"

When we reach my house, Billy waves me off, saying, "I'll be back around 6:00."

***

The tide has receded some, but not enough for us to climb the rocks to search for clues. An older couple sits in beach chairs near the water, holding hands and sipping wine in delicate glasses, and one of the cove's residents walks her golden retriever. She smiles and waves at us.

Billy, Angelina, and I lounge some ways behind the old couple, leaning on our elbows in the sand, chatting and munching on some of Izzie's homemade chocolate-chip brownies. I also have two big ham sandwiches, apples, more brownies, and a thermos of coffee for Harry, compliments of Izzie.

I asked her about him, and she told me she has been feeding him, but it would be a big help if we'd take him his meals once in a while. "It won't hurt you kids to talk to someone like Harry. It'll be a good experience for you. Be respectful," she warned, shaking a long finger at me. "That poor soul has been through a lot."

"Nessie won't come tonight," I say, "not with all these people around."

"That's okay. Maybe she'll be here in the morning. Let's go find Harry." Billy says.

Angelina takes the last bite of her brownie, wiping the crumbs off her jeans as she stands up. "That's the best brownie I've ever had," she says, licking her lips. "Where did you get them?"

"Izzie made them. She makes the best cookies and stuff in town." I'm always happy to talk about Izzie's baking.

THE SECRET OF THE SEA

We pack up and head to Heisler Park, Harry's usual hang-out spot. Poor old Harry. People usually smell him before they see him. Maybe I'll bring him some soap and a towel next time. No. That might be rude. I'd better ask Izzie about it. We find him huddled papoose-like on a bench in front of his regular sleeping spot behind the barbeques. He smells like week-old garbage, but Billy and I try not to let him see we're breathing through our mouths. His greasy hair straggles down the side of his face, colliding with a patchy old beard holding the remains of whatever he's eaten in the last two years, his clothes unrecognizable, though they might have once been pants and a sweatshirt.

"Hi, Harry," I say.

His red-watery eyes give me the once-over, settling on my face. "You're Kalysta's daughter, aren't you?" Rotten-teeth breath adds to the general stink. I see the black stubs as he talks.

I blink. "Y-yes," I stammer. "How did you know?"

"You have her eyes," his gruff, cigarette voice blurts out, "deep chestnut flecked with amber. You have her hair coloring, too—dark with streaks of honey. She is beautiful."

"Oh." I don't know how to respond, so I offer, "This is Billy Hernandez and Angelina Price. I'm Arie. We brought you some sandwiches and coffee."

Harry reaches out to shake Billy's hand. I can see Billy struggling with the idea, not wanting to touch those grubby hands but too polite to intentionally offend the old guy. Harry's eyes grow shrewd as he waits to see what Billy will do. Billy finally grabs Harry's hand and gives it a vigorous shake.

"Nice to meet you, sir." Billy keeps the eye contact, and Harry nods his acceptance.

Angelina takes a step back. Luckily, Harry doesn't notice. When he turns his eyes on her, she steps forward and offers her hand and nods. "It's a pleasure, sir."

I hand Harry the food and thermos.

"That's mighty kind of you. Your mother used to bring me a sandwich at least once a day. You kids have a seat, keep old Harry company for a while. Then you can take the thermos back to Izzie."

"How well do you know Izzie?" I ask, as Billy and I take a seat, one on either side of him. Angelina remains standing in front of Harry.

"I know just about everyone and everything that goes on around here. Izzie and I went to school together," he calmly informs us. He takes a gargantuan bite out of one of the ham sandwiches and slugs it down with coffee, delicately blowing on it first. "She manages to get food to me. That woman has a big heart, almost as big as your mom's. I see her now and then, out in the water. She waves but won't come ashore."

"What?! You've seen my *mom*?" I practically shout, jumping up from the bench like I've been pinched by a crab, almost spilling Harry's coffee. With Harry's head turned toward me, Billy makes cuckoo circles with his finger around his head. I calm down. Billy's right. Harry's what Izzie politely calls eccentric.

"Yeah, every now and then. She's keeping her eye on you, I figure."

"That's a nice thought, Harry," I say, struggling to keep my sarcasm from leaking out. Stung with sadness and humiliation, I slump back down in my seat and stare out at the sea. Keeping an eye on me?! Not one word from her in all these years, but Harry thinks she's watching out for me. Fat chance.

"Your mom has the biggest heart of anyone I've ever known. Too nice for this lousy world. I don't blame her for not coming in from the water." Harry takes another huge bite.

Right. Her heart isn't even big enough for her own daughter. I cross my arms, trying to keep *my* heart from bursting.

"Hey, Harry, have you seen anyone writing in the sand in Fisherman's Cove?" Billy asks.

"Lots of people write in the sand," he answers, taking another big bite.

Billy glances at me, a question in his eyes. I nod back.

"Someone's been writing Arie's name there and this morning left an abalone pearl," Billy tells him.

"Hmmm, well, now, that's an interesting story," he says. "You'll find out in due time."

"What do you mean by that?" I demand, sitting up straight, my eyes boring into his. "Find out what?"

"I mean just what I said. You'll find out when the time is right." He folds the rest of his sandwiches into the paper sack, takes a last slug of coffee, and hands back the thermos. "Thank Izzie for me," Harry says, staring vacantly out at the sea. "I appreciate you kids taking time to talk to a sorry piece of work like me. You'd better get on home before your folks start to worry. It's getting dark now."

"Okay, Harry," Billy says, waving goodbye as we leave.

I walk fast, trying to hold back the tears. "What a waste of time," I snort. "Talking in riddles."

"Maybe he *does* know something," Billy says.

"Sure," I fume, "and I suppose you still believe in Santa Claus."

"I agree with Billy," Angelina adds. "He sees a lot, living like he does. We should pursue that lead."

I wondered when the detective in her would get to work, but Harry doesn't know fantasy from reality. But I keep quiet, afraid I'll shatter like glass if I talk.

"Maybe it *is* your mom," Angelina ventures.

"So what if it is?" I manage to say with just the right amount of mockery and bitterness.

Billy goes quiet, knowing not to pursue an idea when I'm riled. Then he says, "I'm sorry about that with your mom, Arie. He's just a crazy old guy. I've seen him talk to the lamp post, just like my Uncle Al. Don't let it bother you."

"I won't," I manage to say.

Later, in bed, I let the tears come until I fall asleep.

Chapter 6

The next morning, my name is there again, this time with two slightly larger pearls tucked into a shell. I pick them up and hold them to the light. They are so beautiful with the sun shining on their swirling, iridescent colors. We search the rocks and the sand, but there is no sign of anyone.

A splash gets our attention, and there's Nessie, just a few yards out, rolling on her back, then flipping around like a drama queen, making us laugh.

"I bet she knows who left the pearls, if only she could talk," I murmur.

"Nessie, the talking seal—she'd be a big hit at Sea World," he jokes.

I humph in response. The entire class went on a field trip to Sea World last year. I didn't like it, all those beautiful dolphins and orcas penned up—especially the seals with their piercing, intelligent eyes. Everyone laughed at the animal shows, but they made me sad. When I'm a marine biologist, I'm going to try to put a stop to that.

After Nessie back-flips and disappears, we hurry home. Billy doesn't walk with me. He forgot his *Julie of the Wolves* project and had to rush to his house. We're supposed to work on them in class.

"Thanks for scrubbing out the thermos, Sugar Plum." Izzie hunches over the plants in the front yard, picking off little green worms. "How's Harry?" she asks, straightening up and rubbing her back.

"He seemed okay. He ate one sandwich and saved the other. He told me to thank you for him. Would it be rude if I took him some soap and a towel?"

"I think he'd take it kindly, Arie. I'll put some things together for him. I gave him some soap and razor a while back, but he might have left them somewhere and the police found them. They come through here every now and then, gathering up and throwing out all the homeless people's things." She clicks her tongue in her that's-such-a-shame way.

"Why do they do that?" I ask. "He's not hurting anyone."

"I know, Sugar Plum, but some people don't like the homeless in their towns. Unfortunately, it's not the prettiest side of human nature."

"Oh," I reply. "Did you really go to school with him?"

"Yes, but that was a long time ago." She wipes her hands on her apron, opens the screen door, and shoos me inside.

"What was he like?" I follow Izzie to the kitchen.

"He was handsome and quite brilliant. But when he grew up, he began seeing things and talking to people who weren't there. They diagnosed him with schizophrenia. Do you know what that means?" She begins unloading the dishwasher.

"Uh-huh. Billy's uncle has it. He's in a home where they take care of him." I grab an apple out of the fruit basket and take a juicy bite.

"Oh, that's too bad. It must be hard on his family," she says.

"Billy's dad visits him once a week, and sometimes, if he's feeling okay, he comes to their house for holidays."

"The poor soul." She hands me a stack of plates, and I start to put them away in between apple munches.

"Why isn't Harry in a home?" I ask.

"He tried that, but it only made things worse. None of the medications seemed to help. He said he'd rather live by the ocean and talk to the seagulls."

I hesitate, unsure how to tell Izzie about last night. "He says he sees my mom in the water," I finally blurt out.

"Oh, dear, that must have upset you, Arie. I'm so sorry." She stops pulling dishes out of the dishwasher and turns to me. "Pay no attention to him. His hallucinations are real for him, so he does see her, but it's all inside his head. He means no harm." Izzie frowns, her brows scrunched together like a long caterpillar across her forehead.

"That's okay. I know he doesn't mean it. I better get ready for school."

Izzie pulls me in for a hug, and then tells me to scoot.

***

The next morning at the cove, Billy and I scan the sand, and sure enough—my name is written in the same elegant letters with a shell at the end, but this time cradling *three* glossy abalone pearls, swirling with blues and greens and silver. I pick them up, rolling them in my hand, closing my eyes as if these small, misshapen globes held the answers—if I could just remember.

"Wow!" Billy utters, in a reverent tone. "Whoever left these must be a really good diver. Abalone pearls are hard to find."

I'm shivering, even though it's warm this morning.

"You look scared. Are you all right, Arie?" Billy looks at me, one eye squeezed shut against the bright sun.

"Yeah. I'm not scared, just . . . it's so strange and confusing . . .."

A huge *whoosh* close to shore startles us. "Nessie!" I forgot to look for her. I peer at her, searching for the key to the puzzle in her eyes.

"I wish she really *could t*alk," I grumble, both sad and irritated. Billy doesn't joke this time. Nessie rises out of the water, seeming to search my eyes back, her expression as sad as I feel, a longing, an emptiness I can't explain.

We watch her as she dives in one spot, only to emerge somewhere else like that mole-in-the-hole game. We wave and call her name, but she ignores us.

An eternity later, she performs a half-hearted back flip and disappears. I pocket the pearls.

Billy wants to race home, but I don't feel like it. We trudge up the winding hills, the mystery dragging down my mood. Dad's Prius is in the driveway. I'm relieved he's home, though I don't know why. He's on the porch, waiting, dressed in his professor clothes: jeans, a shirt and tie, and a tweed jacket with loafers. Izzie teases him, calling him a cliché, from his clothing to his absent-mindedness, but I think he's handsome.

"Hello there, Billy." Dad waves as we open the gate.

"Hi, Mr. McGinnis!" Billy waves back.

"I'm happy to see you going to the cove with Arie, Billy. I don't like her to go alone."

"*Dad!*" I blush in embarrassment. "I'm not a baby."

"You'll always be my baby, sweetheart. It doesn't hurt to have a friend along, Arie," Dad preaches. "There is safety in numbers. I'm leaving for a mythology conference in the morning. I'll feel better if you're not roaming about on your own. And stay out of that water. It's not safe."

I roll my eyes.

"I'll watch out for her," Billy says in his serious way.

I fire him a killer look. He has the sense to give me a sheepish I'm-sorry, sidelong glance.

"You're a nice young man, Billy. If you kids want a ride to school, you'd better hurry."

"I think we'll walk, Dad," I blurt before Billy can accept. I've had enough humiliation for one day.

"All right, then, but don't be late for school. And Arie, I want to talk to you when I get home tonight."

"Okay, Dad," I reply, mystified. He gathers his briefcase, his feet crunching in the rocky driveway as he walks to his car.

"What do you think he wants to talk about?" Billy wonders aloud.

"Beats me." I head inside and to my room. "I guess I'll find out tonight." I reach under the bed where I keep my shell-covered treasure box, the kind they sell in the local souvenir shops downtown and put the pearls in the secret compartment. I tuck it back behind a box of clothes I've outgrown.

"Don't forget your report," Billy shouts from the living room. I grab my backpack and make a beeline for the kitchen to pick up my lunch. Izzie hands each of us a homemade breakfast sandwich to eat on the way—eggs and cheese on an English muffin.

"Thanks, Izzie!" Billy says, while I give her a quick hug.

Munching on his sandwich, mouth full, Billy asks, "What's up with your dad and the ocean?"

"I wish I knew," I say, taking a mouthful of egg sandwich. "I think it has something to do with Mom, but I'm not sure. We used to all go to the beach together when I was little."

"Are we still going to take surfing lessons this summer?" Billy polishes off his breakfast in one last big bite.

"Of course! Hey, you're not backing out, are you?"

"No way! But are you sure you want to do this without asking your dad?"

"I don't like to lie to him, but he'll tell me no. I just *have* to learn to surf!" I exclaim.

"Okay, Arie, but you'll get in a lot of trouble if he finds out."

"I don't care," I pout. "It'll be worth it."

"I hope you're right. What are you going to do about the consent form?"

"I've been practicing Dad's signature." The statement hangs in the silent air.

Billy stops and gives me the once over. Finally, with a tinge of admiration in his voice, he says, "Aren't you the little forger. Let's hope you don't get caught."

He takes off running and the race is on. Billy wins this time.

Chapter 7

The pungent smell of burnt cheese greets me at the door. Oh no! Dad's cooking. He comes out of the kitchen wearing Izzie's apron, wiping his hands on a towel.

"Hi Dad!" I try to sound enthusiastic but don't succeed. Dad's the worst cook. Izzie says he's the only person she knows who manages to burn water. "Where's Izzie?" I grab a banana out of the fruit bowl to pacify my disappointment—and my stomach.

"I sent her home early. I wanted us to have supper together, just the two of us."

I give him a wry smile and wrinkle my nose, sniffing the smoky air.

"But I thought you loved my grilled cheese sandwiches." He slumps, turning down his mouth, faking hurt feelings.

"Sure, Dad. I love everything you burn."

"Okay, young lady. No dessert for you," he says in his not-really-mad voice.

"What is it? Burnt ice cream?"

He snaps the dish towel at me and misses.

I get the paper plates and plastic forks we use when Izzie isn't here out of the pantry and set the table, complete with paper napkins. Dad pulls a salad out of the fridge. At least he can't burn salad. He gives it a toss with ranch dressing and sets it on the table, along with the stinky grilled cheese disasters, neatly sliced into triangles. I take a wedge, pulling off the burnt-beyond-saving crusts, tear apart what's left, and mix it in with the salad Dad scoops onto my plate.

"So, how's school?" he asks, taking a bite out of his sandwich. The look on his face is priceless. "You're right." Sounding resigned to his poor culinary skills, he slaps his onto his plate and reaches for the dressing.

"Great! Next week we give our oral reports on *Julie of the Wolves*. School will be out soon. I can't wait!" I beam at him and shovel in a bite of salad and burnt cheese smothered in dressing.

"Hmmm," he says, staring off into space.

We eat in silence for a while, and then Dad puts down his fork.

"I've something to talk to you about." He clears his throat.

I wait, expectant, my head cocked like a curious crow.

"How would you like to live on a small ranch?"

I stop, fork in midair, and stare at him. "A ranch? In Laguna Beach?"

"Not in Laguna." He reaches over and retrieves a manila folder off an empty chair.

I hadn't noticed it before. He takes a pile of glossy colored photos out, laying them in a neat row on the table.

"Doesn't this look fun? See the barn in the background?" He slides one of the pictures my way and points to a small, red structure behind and to the right of a sprawling one-story ranch house painted dark blue with cream trim nestled in the emerald grass, surrounded by oak trees. An arch of purple wisteria graces the front gate, softening the wrought iron spikes visible on the fence. It looks like a postcard.

Tucking my knees under me, I rise in the chair, leaning over for a better angle, suspicious and wary. He turns the pictures toward me for inspection. There's a close-up of the interior of the barn, complete with bales of hay, hooks on the walls filled with shovels and other farm tools, a straw-covered floor— and a small brown and white horse munching a carrot Dad's holding. His face grins back at me, his eyes filled with an excitement I've never seen, the usual sadness of his features vanishing in the crooked smile aimed at the camera.

My stomach does an uneasy flip-flop.

"Dad. Where is this place?" My voice sounds far away, unreal, dreading his answer.

"Of course, the horse doesn't come with the property, but you can pick one out," he says, ignoring my question. "Won't that be nice, a horse all your own?"

He's staring in rapture at the pictures, not even looking at me.

"*Dad.* Where is it?" I ask, drawing each word out slowly for emphasis like I'm talking to a small child.

Still avoiding my eyes, his puppy-like enthusiasm dampened, he answers.

"Bloomington, Indiana."

The name drops with a dull thud, a stink bomb ready to explode. A throbbing hammers my temples. "Indiana? I blurt out, "Dad! Are you *kidding* me?! You want to *move*? To Indiana? You can't be serious. We can't leave Laguna Beach." I try to sound mature and practical, but it comes out in a high-pitched screech.

"Now, Arie, I knew you'd be upset, but you'll love it there. There will be snow at Christmas, and we can live on a small ranch with horses and dogs.

You've always wanted a dog. And a cat, as long as it sleeps in the barn." He adds the cat as an afterthought.

"You think you can bribe me with a *dog*?!" My words sound like a swarm of angry bees. "And I don't care about any stupid snow." I throw down my fork. The plastic makes a dull click on the table.

He rushes on while I stare at him in disbelief, my mouth hanging open.

"I've been offered a position at the University of Indiana. It's a great opportunity to head the department and work on my research. I looked at this property a couple of months ago," he says. "I hope it's still available. There's a nice private school near the university for you. I've already spoken with them. You can start in the fall."

He's already decided. I'm so angry and hurt. How could he look at property and find another job without talking to me first? Am I just an afterthought like the cat?

"I don't want to go to a private school in the middle of nowhere!" I cry.

"Be reasonable, honey," he coaxes. "I know it seems like the end of the world now, but you'll make new friends."

"You don't know *anything*!" I shout, pushing back my plate and jumping up from the table. My heart's in my gut, doing a furious tap dance.

"Now, Arie, think about it. We'll have plenty of land for vegetables and flowers—I know how much you like to plant things and watch them grow," he wheedles, all sweet and sickening.

I shoot back, "I like growing things with IZZIE! And there's no *ocean* or *beach* in Indiana. I can't be a marine biologist in stupid *Indiana*. You can't make me go!" Panic battles with fury.

He sits there, giving me his pathetic, sad look. Then I see it in his eyes.

"You want to take me away from the ocean because you *hate* it and Mom *loved* it. That's it, RIGHT?" I glare at him, and his startled expression confirms my suspicions.

"I won't leave Izzie and Billy! And Angelina and my school and the ocean and Nessie. I won't! You can't *make* me!" I'm screaming now, my tears blurring his face. I turn and run to my room and slam the door, flinging myself onto the bed, hugging my pillow to my face. I sob in gulps until my chest feels like a bruised peach. I hear the clatter of the burnt cheese pan and swoosh of water as Dad cleans up.

It's then I realize I'd mentioned Nessie, letting the secret slip. Too bad. If he asks who Nessie is, I won't tell him.

I send Billy a furious text.

MY DAD WANTS TO MAKE ME MOVE TO INDIANA!!

What?!! Call me.

I listen for Dad and hear the television. Good. It's safe to call. Billy answers on the first ring.

"What am I going to do?" I wail. "I can't move to Indiana!"

"I don't believe it! Why does he want to *move*?" Billy asks, sounding as frantic as I feel.

"Something about his stupid job and living on a ranch. But that's not why. He's hated it here since Mom ran away." I'm leaking now from my eyes and nose and mop it up with the sleeve of my sweatshirt, too upset to go to the bathroom for a tissue. "If she hadn't left, this wouldn't be happening. It's all *her* fault!"

"We have to do something to change his mind!"

"Yeah, but *what*?

"I don't know, but we'll think of a plan."

That's Billy—always hatching ideas.

"Do you know where your mom went? Maybe she can help," Billy suggests.

"No, and Dad won't talk about her." I feel all funny inside. Billy has never asked about Mom before. "Besides, she doesn't want me or she'd be here. You know I haven't seen her since I was five."

"True, but you never know. It's worth a try. If she is the mystery writer, then maybe she's back and wants to see you but is afraid you'll be mad. Maybe you can ask Izzie if she knows anything."

I sit quiet for a minute, biting my lip. What if I do find Mom and she doesn't want to see me? After all, she left me. Maybe she won't have anything to do with me. And I *am* mad at her.

I'll just have to risk it. I sit up straight, desperate and determined. If Dad thinks I might move in with Mom, then maybe he won't go to Indiana.

"Arie?"

"Yeah, I'm here. That's not a bad idea. Izzie might know something. I'll meet you at the cove in the morning," I say, and we hang up. I set my fuzzy alarm clock to a low purr so it doesn't wake Dad in the morning. Grabbing my pajamas, I listen at the door. The coast is clear, so I slip out of my room and down the hall.

As the electric toothbrush buzzes away at my teeth, I catch my reflection in the mirror. I rinse and study my face, trying to see Mom in the brown eyes that stare back. Do I really look like her? It seems hopeless and scary trying to find her. Maybe I'm the reason she left. She might tell me to go away and leave her alone.

I guess I'll find out—if I can find her.

I tiptoe back to my room and quietly pack my backpack with everything I'll need for school in the morning. Though it's still early, I flip off my light so

Dad will think I'm asleep. I open my Kindle to read until the TV clicks off, and I hear the soft pad of Dad's loafers coming down the hall. He stops outside my door and softly knocks, so I shove the Kindle under my pillow and hide under the covers, faking sleep.

"Arie? Can I come in, sweetie?"

He eases open the door and comes to my side. When he gently brushes the hair off my face and pulls the blanket tighter over me, I almost cave in and give him a big hug. He kisses me lightly on the forehead and leaves.

I wait until I hear him snoring then crawl under the bed to retrieve my jewelry box from its hiding place, using my cell phone as a flashlight. I sit on the bed, fingering the beautiful pearls, rubbing them between my palms, their silky smoothness haunting me. There's a splinter of memory about their feel, but I can't quite work it out of my mind. Why do they seem so familiar, such a good fit in my hands? There's a glimpse of a string of them, dangling just out of reach of my chubby baby hands. The memory struggles briefly to the surface but disappears into the shadows.

I dig around in my nightstand and find the small black velvet bag that held the locket Dad gave me for my tenth birthday, the locket lost long ago. I carefully drop the pearls one by one into its smooth blackness, tying the ribbon tight and putting it under my pillow.

***

After a fitful night's sleep, I hear the soft purr of the alarm. I dress in silence, carefully tuck the bag of pearls into the zippered pocket of my board shorts, and tip-toe into the kitchen. Ever since I was old enough to write, when Dad was leaving town, I'd stick an I-love-you note on the refrigerator. But not this time. Let him think about *that* while he's on his stupid trip! I stuff a bagel into my backpack, flip my arms through the shoulder straps, grab a banana, and slink out the door.

Guilt bites at me like a determined mosquito. Dad looked so happy in those pictures. But my own bitterness plays tug-of-war at the thought of leaving Laguna Beach. Why can't he be happy here? Why am I not enough?

Maybe it's a girl. The postcard, his goofy grin, it all adds up. He loves his job at the university. Why else would he possibly want to move to the middle of nowhere? He can't hate the ocean *that* much.

Standing at the edge of the ocean in my bare feet, I gaze up at the moon, a pale glimmer in the overcast, not-quite-light sky. Billy won't be here for another half an hour. I peel off my sweatshirt and step out of my shorts, tossing them onto the sand behind me. I let the waves gently lap my toes for what seems like forever, lost in my own sorrows. The water is cold but slightly warmer than the air as I ease farther in, up to my swimsuit. A slight movement several yards ahead interrupts my gloomy thoughts. Nessie. Like a dream, she seems to beckon me. I inch my way into the water, afraid to startle her.

She comes closer, heading straight for me.

All the way in now, I begin to swim, thinking only of Nessie. My body comes alive like an electric current shooting through me. When I'm within a few feet of her, I stop, my heart in my throat, dog-paddling to hold my place. She circles me, inching closer and closer. A streak of velvet slides across my legs, smooth as the bag I put the pearls in.

Suddenly, she springs up, her face a few inches from mine, stopping my breath. Her chocolate eyes melt into mine. That same connection I felt the first time I saw her flows between us. Nudging closer, she presses her wet nose to my forehead, the ocean smell of her filling my senses, her caress an unexpected but welcome warmth. I reach out, careful, and softly place my hand to the side of her whiskered, beautiful face. Slowly, I stroke her sleek head. She nuzzles into my hand. We stay that way, time standing still. I move my hand down the back of her neck and imagine her purring like a kitten. We begin to swim, and I dive under with her, feeling super-charged with strength and agility.

Nessie dives deeper, and I follow. Then she shoots to the surface, dolphin-like. I gather my knees to my chest, using them to jump-start me to the top, my body lunging halfway out of the water, right next to her. Wow! Can humans do that? I didn't even need to hold my breath.

Something strange and miraculous is happening. With my hand on her head, I marvel at the power running through me and the bond I share with this fabulous creature.

Suddenly, she stiffens and turns toward the shore.

"Hey, Arie!!"

Billy's shout breaks the magic spell. Nessie glides away in silence. My salty tears mix with the salt of the sea.

I wave at Billy to signal I'm okay and begin the swim to shore with a heavy heart and limbs.

As I slosh my way out of the water, Billy has my towel ready. "Are you crazy, going in the water alone?" he bristles.

"I'm fine!" I say, yanking the towel out of his hands, hating my bratty tone but unable to help it, so agitated am I at his interruption. "You're not the boss of me."

"I'm sorry." He hangs his head a little.

"Sorry I snapped at you," I relent. It's impossible to stay mad at Billy. "I was with Nessie," I say, almost whispering. The thought soothes my injured soul.

"You swam with the seal?! Wow. That's so cool. Weren't you afraid?"

"It's *Nessie,* and you scared her away." The chilly air turns my skin to goosebumps. I wrap the towel around me and sit knees to chin. Billy looms over me. "Nessie wouldn't hurt me," I say with certainty.

"You don't know that. She's a wild animal," he replies, trying to sound reasonable.

"I *do* know, and besides, you tried to swim with her the first time you saw her last summer," I point out. "But she didn't want to swim with *you.*"

"Oh. Yeah. I forgot." He has no answer to my logic, so he sits beside me in the sand, crossing his arms over the top of his knees. We study the ocean in the early light, watching for Nessie, even though I know she's gone. I wonder where she goes when she's not in the cove.

The hazy sun has risen, turning the clouds to a bruised blue. Billy picks up a muscle shell and lobs it into the water, its soft plunk loud against the barely perceptible waves. He looks around for another missile.

"Look!" Billy jumps up and points down the beach. A shell the size of my palm nestles in the sand next to my name, its precious cargo glistening in the dewy light.

I clutch the towel around me, and join Billy, who has already reached the spot. Crouching down, I pick up the gift—four pearls. A sense of warmth and comfort oozes from them, a reaction I can't explain. I smile up at Billy, who's studying my face.

"You're not freaked out that it might be some sicko stalker?"

"No. It used to scare me a little but not anymore. I don't know why. I just know. I think if anyone wanted to hurt me, they would have by now."

"If you say so," says Mr. Skeptical.

"I'm going to the bathroom to change my clothes." I put the pearls with the others in their velvet pouch, grab my backpack, and slip on my flip-flops.

"I'll walk with you. What was it like, swimming with Nessie?"

"Beyond awesome." I shiver in delight at the memory.

"How close did she get?"

"She swam right up and kissed my forehead with her nose."

"No *way.* Did she, really?" Wonder fills his voice.

"Her whiskers felt like hairbrush bristles, but her nose was soft. It was like a fairytale." We reach the restrooms, so I go in to dry off and change back into my dry clothes, brush my teeth and hair, and join Billy, who's sitting on the bench above the cliffs. Billy shares my bagel and banana and we head to school. I text Izzie so she can let Dad know I'm okay. I don't need him sending out a posse to look for me because he thinks I'm a baby who can't take care of herself.

Despite my stormy emotions, the magic of Nessie stays with me, bringing the hope of impossible things.

Chapter 8

After school, Billy, Angelina, and I stop by my house to load up our backpacks with whatever treats Izzie has prepared. The small suitcase she brings when Dad's out of town almost blocks the door.

"Izzie, I'm home."

"No need to state the obvious, girl. I heard you all the way down the block." She comes out of Dad's room carrying a pile of sheets, tosses them into the laundry basket waiting in the hall, and gives my head a good rustling. "What are you kids up to today? Heading to the cove, I assume?"

"Yep!" I reply, my dark mood barely veiled.

"There's yogurt and fruit for the three of you, plus Harry's dinner."

"Awww, Izzie, no cookies?" Billy gives her an exaggerated pout.

"One apiece. Your teeth are all going to rot out of your heads if you keep eating so much sugar."

Billy perks up. "Thanks, Izzie."

We stuff the packages into our packs.

"Be home before dark, Arie," Izzie warns. "I promised your dad."

The dark cloud loses its thin veil, thickening like a tempest at the mention of Dad.

Izzie looks thoughtfully at me. "Cheer up, Sugar Plum. Tonight, we'll have a long talk, just the two of us."

"Okay," I reply, my shoulders slumped.

On the way to the beach, Angelina asks in her blunt way, "What's wrong? Was there a pea under your mattress, princess?"

I bark a bitter laugh. Billy and I tell Angelina about Dad's plan to ruin my life.

"No *way!*" she protests, shaking her head. "Can you talk him out of it?"

"I don't know," I say, fighting back tears. "He's found a house and school already. He didn't even ask me what I thought!"

"Parents rarely ask us what we think," she replies.

"We're trying to think of a plan. Any ideas, detective?" Billy asks.

"Let's keep working on finding the mystery writer. There might be something there to use as leverage." Angelina sounds so determined it gives me a slice of courage.

"Thanks, but I doubt that'll help." I run my fingers through my hair, just like Dad does, then quickly smooth it back down.

"She's gonna ask Izzie about her mom," Billy tells Angelina. "We hope she can help."

Angelina doesn't respond right away, but then asks, "Do you know where she is? I thought she left a long time ago, like my dad."

My chest tightens, but Angelina knows how I feel. Her dad ran away, too. I still feel awkward talking about Mom, but I say with more confidence than I feel, "Izzie knows almost as much as Harry about what happens in Laguna Beach. If anyone knows where Mom is, it's Izzie." To end the questions, I shout, "Let's race!" Billy and Angelina have no choice but to chase after me.

It's a drizzly day, and the tide is out, so we visit Fisherman's Cove first. Angelina spies it this time—my name in the wet sand. We abandon our packs in the sand and run to the spot.

I drop down on my knees, lightly tracing the letters with my finger, the delicate curve of the lines, and pick up four more pearls. Pulling the velvet pouch from my pocket, I add the new ones to the hoard—fourteen pearls. Billy and Angelina form a circle with me, all eyes on the open bag of treasures.

"Wow, they're beautiful, Arie. Can I touch them?" Angelina holds out her cupped hands, and I slide the pearls out in a gleaming stream. She rolls them around, savoring their feel, then hands them back. I tie them into their bag and put it in my zipper pocket.

"I've never found anything here during the afternoon before, only the morning." I ponder this new development. How would the mystery sand-writer know I would get them before someone else did?

"And you have no idea who's doing this?" she asks.

"Not a clue," Billy answers for me.

"Billy," Angelina's face lights up, her eyes bright with excitement, "give me your cell phone."

Billy hands it over, and we watch as she turns on the camera and takes pictures of the writing.

"My mom lets me use hers sometimes," she smiles with confidence, clicking away from different angles. "Email those to me and I'll print them out at school tomorrow."

"Why?" I ask, intrigued.

"I'll match it and find out whose sand-writing that is. Does it always look the same?"

"Yes, but I don't see how you're going to find the person's handwriting. It could be anybody," doubting-face Billy says.

Angelina gives him a don't-be-so-dumb look. "No, smarty-pants; it's *obviously* someone who knows Arie. So that narrows it down. I have a hunch that the lady in white that Trevor saw might know something."

"What do you mean?" I ask, not seeing a connection.

"Just email me those pictures. I don't want to say anything else until I'm sure." She smiles mysteriously. "It might lead nowhere, but it's worth a try."

"Okay, Hannah West, girl detective," I say, knowing Angelina loves the Hannah West stories.

We hang around in the cove for a while, watching for signs of the mystery writer, chucking random shells into the water, and searching the tide pools in the rocks that lead to Shaw's Cove. Orange dinner-plate-sized starfish dot the rocks, clinging like Velcro, waiting for the tide to turn. Tiny hermit crabs dart around, tucking their heads into their stolen shells like turtles whenever we pick them up. Billy finds a baby octopus hiding in a miniature cave in the side of one rock and pokes gently at it with a piece of driftwood.

"Stop that, you idiot! You know you're not supposed to mess with the marine life. This cove is a preserve." I fume at him, giving him the stink-eye.

"I'm not hurting it, Sergeant Killjoy. I'm studying it," he replies, all haughty, still poking the poor creature.

"Then study it with your eyes," I say, yanking the stick out of his hand.

"Okay, okay! Sheesh."

Changing the subject, Billy says, "Arie and I are going to take surfing lessons, if Arie can figure out how to forge her dad's signature."

"I've been practicing, but I'm not very good at it yet," I admit.

"I can do it for you. I've been signing Mom's name for years because she always forgets to sign the consent forms. She doesn't mind," Angelina casually states.

Billy and I stare at Angelina with new respect. Then I remember that Angelina has the best handwriting in class. I've seen her perfectly imitate the teacher's handwritten notes on the board. How had I forgotten that? "You think you can sign my dad's name?"

"Sure. Just bring me something he's signed, and I'll practice." She replies, as if it's no big deal to regularly forge adults' signatures.

"I have an idea!" Billy practically shouts, like he's just developed the internet or something. "Why don't you take lessons with us? Arie and I have saved more than enough from our allowances and chores to pay for yours, and it can be a thank-you."

I could kiss Billy right now.

"That costs too much money. I can't let you do that," she protests, reluctance battling with the longing in her voice.

"Oh, pleeease!" I beg. "It would be a lot more fun if you learn to surf, too."

"I don't think I should," she replies, tossing her blond hair.

"Come on, Angelina!" Billy says, in his insistent, sometimes bossy way. "It'll be fun."

"We'll just keep bugging you until you say yes." I stare her down.

"Okay," she relents, "if it gets you two off my back."

I give her an enthusiastic hug.

"We'd better find Harry before it gets dark," Billy reminds us.

We make our way along the winding path above the beach where the homeless hang out, searching for Harry.

We find him perched on the bench next to the path right before Main Beach. He's wearing Dad's old sweatshirt Izzie gave him and talking to no one. "I'll keep your secret, don't worry about that," Harry says.

"Whose secret?" Billy asks, startling poor old Harry, who nearly falls off the bench.

"Never you mind. And don't sneak up on an old man like that. You about gave me a heart attack." His milky eyes nervously wander from us to the ocean.

"Sorry, sir," Billy replies, but his tight lips and bright eyes tell me he's suppressing a laugh.

I hand Harry his dinner and ask, "Have you seen the lady in white recently? I've been trying to find out who she is."

"I see her from time to time," Harry replies, opening the bag of food and nosing around, sniffing. "Smells good." He closes the bag and sits there, saying nothing. His face goes blank as he stares listlessly out at the ocean.

I try to draw him back to reality, pleading, "Harry, if you know who the lady in white is, please tell me. You said I'd find out in good time, but I've just got to know. My dad plans to make me move at the end of the summer."

In response, Harry croons in his cigarette voice, sounding more like a bullfrog than a man:

> Summer has come,
> Loudly sing cuckoo!
> Seeds grow, and meadow blooms
> And the woods bud anew,
> Sing cuckoo!

Angelina leans over and whispers, "He's cuckoo, all right!"

"Come on, Harry, this is important. We need to know who she is." Billy's voice comes out tinged with irritation.

Harry continues singing, lost in his imagined world.

> Fair lady, you were clad in white
> When first your gentle eyes I met,
> And never shall my heart forget,
> The vision of that August night."

"Harry," Billy says, gently touching Harry's shoulder.

Harry shakes him off like an annoying fly.

"Harry, *please!*" I beg. "I have to know."

"Summer's comin', yes it is. You just wait. August is the answer," he replies to the sea, staring at it as if we don't exist.

"It's no use," I admit, trying to hold back tears. My life is falling apart, and all Harry can do is sing nonsense. That's what I get for talking to a crazy person. "Let's go," I tell Angelina and Billy. I can hear the disgust and defeat in my words.

Time to see if Izzie knows anything.

Chapter 9

When I get home from the beach, the house smells like boiled shrimp and peach pie, my favorites. I toss my backpack on my bed and head to the kitchen. "Boiled shrimp! Thanks, Izzie!"

"Hello, Sugar Plum. I figure you deserve a treat."

"And peach pie and a movie?" I'm practically jitterbugging, my sour mood melting like morning dew. Life doesn't get much better than peach pie and movie night with Izzie. The smell of thyme and tarragon, cayenne pepper and lemon juice compete with the aroma of baked peaches, bring back memories of summers past, helping Izzie peel shrimp and mix the spices.

"And a smidge of vanilla ice-cream. Go wash up and we'll eat," Izzie says, pulling the pie out of the oven.

I set the table while Izzie dishes up juicy shrimp swimming in its tangy, homemade sauce, steamed carrots, and Cajun rice. We sit quiet for a while, intent on our food. I sense Izzie sneaking peeks at me. It makes me awkward, longing to know things but afraid of the answers.

Between bites, Izzie says, "I know you have a lot of questions about your mom. It's time we talked." She waits for a response, her fork held aloft, poised at me like a miniature version of Neptune's trident.

"What do you remember about her," I finally ask, "why she left? Dad gets upset when I talk about her." Bitterness creeps into my voice, and I fight resentment at Dad and Mom.

Izzie raises an eyebrow. She puts down her fork, wipes sauce off her chin, and takes a sip of sweet tea. "That's a big question, honey, but you deserve to know. You're getting to an age when a child would naturally begin to wonder."

"Do you know where she went?" My question hovers in the air while Izzie takes her time. I can practically see her turning the question around in her head, examining it from every angle.

"Not exactly, no," she says, "but I have a feeling she didn't go far."

"Why do you think that?" My heart gives a little skip, and I can barely breathe.

"Things she said to me the night she left." Izzie's words come out a little hesitant.

"What did she say?" I try to sound casual, but Izzie knows me too well.

"Hold your horses, girl, I'll get to all that." She settles back in her chair and into her story. "Your mom is the kindest, most lovely creature I ever met, always willing to help anyone in need. Everyone loved her. Do you remember her at all?"

Yeah, so kind she ran off and left her own daughter to be raised without a mother. "Just a little. Mostly, it's like a faded dream."

Izzie nods as if that makes perfect sense.

I push the rice around on my plate, not wanting to meet Izzie's eyes boring into me like one of Dad's drills.

Finally, I ask, "Was she mad at Dad? Is that why she left?"

Izzie's voice softens. "I don't think your mom is capable of being mad at anyone."

I continue to play hockey with my food. Why is it people keep harping on how great Mom was?

"Would you like to know a little about when I first met her?" Izzie patiently waits for me to think it through.

"I want to know where she is *now*." I sound like a spoiled brat and wouldn't blame Izzie if she sent me to my room, but she gives me her pity face, soft, with one side of her mouth slightly turned up.

"One thing at a time, Arie. You know I need to warm up a little to tell a story."

She asks me what I want to know then won't answer? Adults can be so aggravating. Seeing the moisture in Izzie's bright green eyes, I nod.

"We met at the animal shelter where we both volunteered. That girl sure had a way with animals. They would calm right down when she was around," Izzie says, coughing a little on the Cajun spices.

I asked her one time why she ate fiery seasoning, since it made her choke, and she just grinned and said, "Spicy food for a spicy gal."

"Your mom also volunteered at the teen shelter and fought City Hall to help the homeless." Izzie continues, "She never could stand to see people or animals suffer—especially the animals.

She helped other teenagers but didn't stick around to help her own *daughter*? It's like getting an ice pick through the heart. I cross my arms, and stare into space beyond Izzie's head.

"'Most people make their own problems,' she told me once, 'but animals are at our mercy.' She worked with the marine mammal rescue center, too. I never saw anyone, not even the veterinarians, who understood sea lions and seals the way your mom did. It was almost as if she knew what they were thinking."

I sit sulking with my elbows on the table, my face cupped in my hands.

"One time, the neighbor's tomcat caught a hummingbird," Izzie says, "and your mom yelled at that old cat to drop the bird, and it obeyed, slinking off in apology. She brought that little bird in the house and made a nest in a shoe box to keep it warm. The next day, she took it outside, enclosed in her hands like a prayer, and when she opened them, it flew up into the air, buzzed around her hair as if in thanks, then sped off. She'd sit in the garden, still as a monk, and glittery hummingbirds would land right on her. Squirrels ate out of her hands." Izzie shakes her head in wonder.

I try to connect the Mom images in my head with this new information. She sounds too wonderful to be true.

Because she is. She didn't want *me*.

The angry voice in a small jar hidden in a corner of my mind cracks open its lid, invading my fantasy.

Izzie tilts her head, hesitating as if she's contemplating whether to continue, but says, "You're a lot like her, you know. I see it in how kindly you treat Angelina, and you're always dragging home some injured bird or helping a cat off the roof. Remember that time you found a lizard missing a tail and thought it needed doctoring? You were only six years old. I had to explain to you that lizard tails grow back."

Izzie leans forward, tugging at my elbows, pulling my arms straight toward her, giving them a little shake. "No elbows on the table, young lady," she says, but I know she's fooling around. She's trying to lighten the mood.

"I didn't believe you, so you looked it up on the internet for me." I smile at the memory, shoving the angry voice back into its jar.

"Pretty sad times when a child believes the internet before grown-ups," she huffs.

I giggle and chuck the last shrimp in my mouth.

Izzie smiles a sad smile. "Despite all the happiness she brought others, sorrow hung around her like a cloak. Your dad took her to doctors, but nothing seemed to help. She got better for a while after she had you, but eventually the blues returned."

I rest my elbows on the table again, sobering at the thought it might be my fault she left. "Why was she sad?"

"I don't know, Sugar Plum. Some people just have a bit of darkness in them. They can't help it. It's a little like Harry and Billy's Uncle Al. Let's clean the table while I tell you about the day she left."

We carry everything to the kitchen, and I wipe off the table. Izzie washes while I rinse and dry. We don't use the dishwasher when Dad's away. Izzie says there aren't enough dishes, but I don't mind. I like helping Izzie.

"The day your mom left, I saw a light in those sad eyes that I hadn't seen since the day you were born," Izzie resumes. "It had started raining right before she got to my house. Your dad wasn't home yet from the university. She had wrapped you in her yellow raincoat, leaving only your tiny face uncovered, those big brown five-year-old eyes peering out, looking so frightened. She put you in my arms, her voice trembling as she told me she had to go, that she didn't want to leave but couldn't live without her soul. She asked me to take care of you. 'Promise you'll take care of Aurora,' she pleaded and kissed your forehead. Before I could protest, ask her what she meant, she was gone, running down the steps and into the rain. That was the last time I saw her."

"But *why*? Why did she leave me?" My voice sounds pleading and pathetic. Izzie pulls me in for a bear hug, and I squeak a tiny sob.

"She didn't leave *you*, sweetheart; don't ever think she didn't love you. She left a life she couldn't live. I thought maybe she went back to Ireland, but I got a phone call about a week later telling me not to worry, and that someday she'd explain everything to you. I've gotten two more calls over the years, your mom asking about you, but nothing for the last three."

"What else did she say?" I ask, the desperate words echoing in my ears.

"She said to take care of you, make sure you know she loves you," Izzie says.

"Do you think she'll do it, come back and tell me?"

"I don't know," Izzie considers, speaking slowly and gently, as if she's talking to a frightened animal. "I hope so. She has such a good heart; I know leaving you and your dad was the hardest thing she ever did. Your dad was so devastated I didn't think he'd get through it."

Poor Dad. I hadn't thought too much about how he must have felt. But that doesn't give him the right to move me to the middle of nowhere.

Izzie takes my face in her hands and wipes a single tear off with her thumb. I hate crying. I feel like such a baby.

"I thought maybe I could live with her and stay here so I don't have to go to Indiana," my voice barely whispers.

Izzie smooths my hair in sympathy and then busies herself with pie and ice-cream.

"Let's have some of this peach pie and get comfortable. You pour the milk."

I get the almond milk out of the fridge and pour.

"I think you need to let your mom come to you in her own time," Izzie finally says. "I think she will. Be patient."

"But I need her *now*, before Dad tries to make me go to Indiana!" I try to get a grip on the panic that threatens to destroy me. I almost ask Izzie if I can live with her, but Dad would never let me.

"I know, Arie, but I have a feeling everything will work out all right. Now, what movie do you want to see?"

When Izzie uses that tone, the conversation is over.

I choose *The Secret of Roan Inish,* a fantasy about selkies, Irish mermaids. Izzie falls asleep after an hour, but I'm enchanted by the magical movie. When it's over, I quietly gather up the pie dishes and carry them to the kitchen to wash, thinking about the story, about Fiona and her brother, Jaime, who is lost at sea, and the grown-ups who don't believe her when she says she's seen Jaime in his cradle taken care of by the selkies. I cry at the end when the selkies bring Jaimie safely home to his family.

***

The clink of cup and saucer, the running of water, and the rattle of dishes, tell me Izzie's up. Soon, the smell of fresh coffee has me wide awake. Izzie let me taste it once, but I gagged on its bitterness, even after she put a lot of milk in it. Grownups seem obsessed with the stuff, but it's gross to drink, though I love the smell of it brewing.

I stretch and get up to shower, sensing the fog outside before I see it. It has a way of softening the early morning sounds: the newspaper delivery truck rumbling by, the yap of excited dogs yanking at their owners' leashes, the occasional lonely howl of a coyote hurrying home before full daylight. Fog blankets it all in quiet bliss.

Good. Fog means the cove will probably be empty. Billy and I will have it to ourselves. Maybe I can get there early and swim with Nessie.

When my backpack's ready for school, I stash it by the front door. Billy's sitting on the steps, messing around with his cell phone. I knock on the window. "I'll be right out!" He nods that he's heard, too intent on his game to look up.

Izzie's sitting at the table, sipping coffee and reading *The Los Angeles Times,* two sharpened pencils waiting for her—Izzie loves crossword puzzles and completes one every morning.

She looks up when I come in and pulls her cheater glasses halfway down her nose so she can see me. "You ready for school, Sugar Plum?"

"All packed," I chirp. "Billy's waiting on the porch."

"Why didn't that boy knock on the door? Sitting out there all by himself," she mutters, taking a sip of coffee.

"He probably didn't want to wake you."

"Take him a banana. I'll have breakfast ready when you get back—eggs and oatmeal. And tell Billy no argument." She nudges her glasses in place and goes back to reading. I grab two bananas and join Billy.

"Did you learn anything from Izzie? Does she know where your mom went?" Billy's troubled voice tells me he's worried.

"No, not exactly," I say, using Izzie's words, "but she thinks Mom's not too far away." I don't offer any more information, reluctant to share what little I know with anyone, protecting it like a dragon's hoard. "Izzie will help if she can." I huff out a deep breath and change the subject. "Let's race!"

Billy needs no further encouragement and darts off, me sprinting to catch up with his lead. I pour all my anger, all my resentment into the run—at Dad, at Mom for not being here—pounding the ground in a fury. I zoom past Billy, winning by several yards.

"Wow! You ran like something was chasing you," he says, awed.

"Come on, slowpoke!" I stick out my tongue at him and hurtle down the steps of the cove. "I don't want to miss Nessie."

I'm also hoping to find more pearls. The little gifts make me feel special, somehow, like I matter, something unique meant just for me. I smile at my name and the now-familiar shell of pearls, four again. For a second, I wonder if it could be Mom. But the hope is unbearable, so I shove it aside and gather up the prizes, inspecting each one, then hand them to Billy.

He rubs them clean, brushing off the sand, and then holds the treasures in his palm as if testing their weight. "How many do you have now?"

"These four make eighteen." I pull the pouch out of my pocket and hand it to Billy. He drops them in, one by one, with the rest.

"You almost have enough for a necklace." I can see him thinking as he cups the bag, caressing the velvet between two fingers.

"How many do you think it'll take?"

"About twenty-five, for a short one. I can ask my dad."

"Let's wait and see if I get enough first." I like the thought of wearing them around my neck, close to my skin. I'd never take them off. Billy hands me the bag, and I stash it away, zipping it in tight.

The sun's straining through the fog, a yellow yolk in the sky. I scan the ocean, and there's Nessie, silently watching us, her gaze hypnotic. Yearning to join her, I step toward the water. An invisible rope pulls me to her, the water now up to my waist, plastering my shorts to my skin, my t-shirt cold around my stomach. She swims forward a couple of feet, stops, and raises her body up out of the water, exposing her front fins, then slaps one fin onto the surface of the sea. In imitation, I slap my hand down hard. She slaps back. Soon, we're both slapping the water in unison. Billy, standing ankle-deep in the sea, laughs behind me. Nessie falls backward and tumbles in circles, dives down, then suddenly leaps out of the water, cannon-balling so hard she creates a small wave.

Nessie's so close we can almost touch her. She rises again, alert, looking beyond us. That's when I hear the voices. Billy and I turn to see a couple making their way down the steps. When we glance back at Nessie, she nods her head three times and vanishes beneath the sea. Standing there in my wet clothes, I search the water's surface, feeling forlorn and lost.

Chapter 10

The clock purrs me awake, and I spring out of bed. Saturday! No school and all day at the beach. Angelina and Billy are going to meet me there.

Angelina's mom finally relented to let Angelina come with us to the cove with us in the mornings. Izzie called and talked to her.

I want to get there early to have Nessie all to myself, so I leave Izzie a note and run at top speed, the heavy backpack only slightly slowing my progress. Flying down the stairs, I begin removing the straps and toss the pack at the bottom. Tugging at my sweatshirt, still running, I trip and hit the sand hard, landing in a tangle, but roll right back up. Stripped down to my suit, I enter the water, up to my knees, hardly noticing the cold. My eyes search the surface, hoping to see her, *needing* to see her. It's still not quite light, but at least there's no fog. I swim out a few yards. Still no Nessie. But when I scan the rocks, a dark blob detaches itself from the black inkiness and slides into the water.

Nessie rises next to me, blowing out air in a huff, sprinkling my face with drops of her fishiness. I lean forward and kiss her nose. We begin to swim, moving out beyond the rocks where I've never swum before. But I'm not afraid, not with Nessie next to me.

My chest tingles, and my body feels sleeker, stronger than ever. When Nessie dives under, I dive with her, deeper and deeper, oblivious to the cold. As we glide along in the dark depths, I find I'm not struggling to hold my breath. And despite the darkness, my eyes can make out the shapes of the mussel-crusted rocks, kelp floating like mermaid's hair, and a bat ray swimming lazily by beneath us. A small leopard shark startles me, but I relax, remembering they're not dangerous to humans unless provoked, but then I wonder if it can hurt Nessie. I search for her but don't see her. I jet torpedo-like to the surface.

Stopping to catch my breath, I look around for Nessie. Eerie silence floods my senses. "Nessie!" I call out. "Nessie, come back!" I turn in frantic circles, searching.

She bursts out of the water, about twenty yards out. I draw in a deep breath and blow it out in relief. "Nessie, you scared me half to death!" Cavorting around me, playful, she ignores my reprimand. Her high spirits infect me, and I reach out to touch her. Her silky wet head, the smell of her—I can't get enough. She leans into my hand, head-butting like a playful cat.

Nessie nudges me toward the shore, so I reluctantly begin the long swim, my playmate following.

When my feet hit the sand, I turn, but Nessie is already heading back to deep water. She raises a flipper as if in salute, backflips, and is gone.

Retrieving my backpack from the sand, I vigorously rub myself with the towel, and struggle into my sweatshirt. Wrapping the towel around my legs, I sit in the sand, waiting for Billy and Angelina. Enthralled by the swim, I hadn't even checked for pearls. I spot them nesting in the sand at the end of my name as usual. I haul myself up, my limbs weak with fatigue, and walk slowly to the spot. Five more exquisite pearls.

Angelina arrives first and sits down next to me in the sand by my name. "More pearls?"

"Five. Now I have twenty-three. Billy says he and his dad can make a necklace out of them for me if I get twenty-five."

"I hope you're right about this mystery person not wanting to hurt you," Angelina says. "It would freak me out."

I can't think of a way to explain how I'm so sure I'm not in danger, so I remain silent.

The sun has risen behind us, warming our backs. We sit for a while, content with each other's company.

"Any luck with the handwriting?" I ask, faking nonchalance, though truthfully, I'm still so wowed by the enchanted morning, I'm not as excited as I should be.

"Not yet, but I have a plan. Next Saturday, I'll go with my mom to her work. She's a clerk in county records," she replies, "so I'll start looking."

"Do you plan on searching all the records until you get a match?" I joke.

She smiles mysteriously. "If that's what it takes."

"Okay, Hannah West, keep your little secret," I say.

"I turned *Nightbird* back in at the library if you want to read it," Angelina informs me.

"Nice job changing the subject!" I toss my head as if miffed, but Angelina just laughs. Billy jogs over the sand, waving. "Sorry I'm late."

Clearly, he's been running; he's all sweaty and winded. "Sleeping in, Sleeping Beauty?" I ask.

"Dad needed me to help with the lawn. What did I miss?"

"Five more pearls," Angelina replies.

"And my swim with Nessie," I say, satisfied by his look of regret.

"When am *I* going to get to swim with her?" he grumbles.

"Never," I smugly reply. "She doesn't want to swim with *you*?"

"I can try."

"Billy Hernandez," I say, standing up, "you leave Nessie alone."

"You don't own her," he says, but his tone is weak. He hates fighting with me. I always win.

"Go ahead and try, then. You'll see. She only wants *me*," I tell him in my haughtiest voice, driving home my point. But really, I'm afraid that I'm not special enough for her to want to swim just with me. I'd be so hurt if she swam with anyone else, especially Billy.

"Certainly, Your Majesty. Your wish is my command." He stands ramrod straight, and bends at the waist in a graceful bow, swishing his ball cap across the sand.

In response, I toss a handful of sand at him, which lands in his hair.

"Hey, cut it out!" he cries.

I just laugh as he tries to brush out the sand with his fingers.

We sit on our towels, facing the ocean. The sun on my numb-from-cold skin is divine. Funny, I didn't feel cold in the water. I don't know what's happening to my body, but I like it. I feel powerful.

As the sun climbs higher, people begin to wander into the cove. Kids search the tide pools and play in the waves while adults read under the shade of umbrellas. One adventurous Labrador retriever leaps into the water after a tennis ball his owner has thrown. It's a perfect day.

The only thing spoiling the fun is Indiana looming in the future. I shove it away. I'll think about it later.

"Is the water cold?" Angelina asks.

Billy and I exchange a look. "It's really quite nice once you get used to it," I fib. Billy gives me the evil eye but doesn't say anything. Angelina takes her shirt and shorts off, revealing a slightly-too-small one-piece blue suit.

"I'll go in with you," Billy volunteers, shedding his sweatshirt.

"I'll stay here and watch. I've had enough swimming for one day." I bite my lip to keep a mischievous smile from giving away the game.

Billy runs for it and dives into a small wave, Angelina right behind him. She explodes out of the water, gasping from the iciness of it, and her high-pitched squeal pierces the air. All the little kids are cracking up and pointing at her.

"Arie!" she shouts, "you little liar!"

I'm laughing so hard my side aches. "It's worth it to see your face!" I shout back. She shivers, drops back into the water, and expertly swims after Billy.

The rest of the morning, we lie on the beach, sunning ourselves like sea lions, chatting and making plans. My cell phone rings, but when I see it's Dad calling, I let it go to voicemail. I stuff it into the bottom of my backpack.

We eat lunch at my house in the backyard garden. Izzie has loaded down the picnic table with a salad of fresh tomatoes picked from the thick vine that grows up the trellis, almost pulling it down with its load of red fruit; tuna salad sandwiches chock full of crunchy mild peppers (also homegrown), onions, and her special blend of spices; and a pitcher of fresh lemonade made from the lemons of the old tree that crowds the whitewashed wooden fence.

The thought of having to leave it all makes my stomach clench into a knot, ruining my appetite. I choke down a few bites in lonely silence. Intent on their lunches. Angelina and Billy don't notice, but Izzie stands in the doorway from the garden to the kitchen, giving me a thoughtful look.

The three of us clean up the mess, putting away extra food in plastic containers, wiping the table, and doing the dishes, flicking sudsy water at each other and snapping towels.

"Okay, you little heathens," Izzie banters, "time to go. I need Arie this afternoon."

I give her a quizzical look and she returns a conspiratorial wink. I wonder what she wants.

After they leave, Izzie turns to me, hands on her hips. "What's this I hear about you ignoring your dad's phone calls?"

I shrink a little inside but stand my ground. "I don't want to talk to him." I clench my jaw and defiantly raise my head, meeting her eye to eye.

"Don't give me that look, missy. I know you're mad at the man, you've a right to be, but as my mama always told me, 'You'll catch more flies with honey.' He handled it badly, for sure, but shutting him out like that won't help matters."

I slump in defeat and begin to cry, quiet tears, with only a sniffle or two, but it melts Izzie, and she puts an arm around me.

"Listen to me, Sugar Plum. The war isn't over yet. Don't lose hope. I think in the end he'll see reason. If not, you'll have to make the best of it. I'll always be here for you, no matter what."

I wipe my eyes with the back of my hand.

"Now go rinse your face," Izzie gently says. "We need to go shopping to buy you bras."

The shock of this statement puts a halt to my crying. "What do you mean, buy me *bras*?"

Izzie looks meaningfully at my white t-shirt. "Have you given yourself a good, long look lately?" she asks, unperturbed by my distress.

I turn and face the hall mirror, glancing down at my chest, two tiny mounds clearly visible in the brightly lit hallway, and I grudgingly admit she's got a point.

Chapter 11

After dragging me through the humiliation of several stores at Fashion Island, Izzie finally loses her patience at Macy's.

"You will pick out five bras and that's final. There must be something here that will suit you."

"They're all girlie and pink with bows and flowers and *lace*. They itch," I whine.

"Look, here's a plain white one," she says, yanking it off the rack. "Not even you can complain." She thrusts the "training" bra into my hands and pushes me toward the dressing room. "Now scoot!"

"I don't know why they call them training bras. What exactly are they training me for?" I grumble. Izzie's amused tsk follows me as I disappear into the dressing room.

I study myself in the full-length mirror, turning to view every angle and then pull my t-shirt on over it. Not bad. At least those bumps don't show so much.

I wish Mom were here.

This unexpected thought gives me a sting of guilt. *She's* the one who left. Dad stayed and took care of me. I should be mad at her, not Dad. Sweet, loveable Dad. Maybe Izzie's right. It's all so confusing. Resolved to try more 'honey' like Izzie says, I tug off the bra with my t-shirt still on and hang it back on its hanger.

When I come out, Izzie is still sorting through the racks, pulling out every plain bra she can find. I end up with three white, one yellow, and one pale blue. She pays for them and sends me back into the dressing room to put one on.

Finally finished, we head home, driving down Pacific Coast Highway with the radio blaring Willie Nelson's "You Were Always on My Mind," one of Izzie's favorite songs. Too tired to cook, Izzie stops for pizza.

We eat on paper plates in front of the TV watching reruns of *The Big Bang Theory*, me cross-legged on the couch, Izzie beside me, her bare feet on the coffee table.

"You wore out my legs, girl," she complains, wiggling her toes and groaning.

My phone rings, insistently jangling into our coach potato laziness. It's Dad. Izzie gives me the arched eyebrow treatment.

"Okay, okay, Izzie," I say, resenting the intrusion but antsy to talk to him. Maybe he's changed his mind. Nervously, I answer.

"Hi, Dad," I say, trying to sound nice but feeling as stiff as a paper doll.

"Hello, sweetheart," he says, his voice tired and sad. "I'm so glad you answered. Are you still mad at me?"

"I don't know," I mumble. "I guess not."

"Let's not fight, Arie. Can we at least agree on that?"

"Okay, Dad."

"I'm sorry I upset you."

The relief in his voice makes me ashamed for being so mean.

"I'm sorry, too," I tell him. "I love you, Dad.

"I love you, too, sweetheart, always."

"Do you still want to move?" I ask, my voice almost a whisper, afraid of the answer.

"Let's talk about it Monday, when I get home," Dad responds, deflated.

We say goodbye and hang up. Izzie nods her approval.

***

On Sunday, Billy and Angelina help me make a quick tour of the beach, but the day is dismal. No Nessie, no Harry, and no Trevor, but five more pearls huddle together in their usual spot next to my name.

"That makes twenty-eight!" Billy announces, "more than enough for a necklace."

"Should I take the pearls to Dad's shop?" Billy asks.

Studying the pearls in their velvet pouch, I'm reluctant to let them go. I gaze out at the grey ocean, as if expecting an answer. Billy and Angelina patiently wait for my decision. Finally, I peer up at Billy, my eyes slit against the peculiar glare that comes with the overcast day. "Can we make the necklace together?"

"I don't want to drill the holes myself. I might break them," he answers, picking a pearl from the bag, thoughtfully rubbing it between his thumb and first finger. "I haven't had much practice yet."

A small smile curls the edges of his mouth, the one he gets when he's figured something out. Full of easy confidence, he drops the pearl back into the bag and gazes at me with his I've-got-an-idea eyes, full of light.

"Let's go to my house. We have a pearl drilling machine at the shop, but Dad has a set of hand tools at home. He'll help us drill the holes," he says, all proud of himself.

I'm proud of Billy, too, but don't say so. His head's already as big as a full moon. "Good idea," I nod, but he knows I'm jittery with excitement.

"You don't mind I told Dad about the pearls?" Billy asks.

"No, I don't mind."

Angelina makes a not-so-subtle clearing of her throat.

Guiltily, we startle. Billy and I had been lost in our own private world, Angelina forgotten. Izzie would say we've 'fallen into bad habits.' It's been just Billy and me since kindergarten. Sometimes, we forget our manners. Angelina crosses her arms over her chest and looks from me to Billy, her eyes full of mischief.

"What?" Billy and I ask, almost in unison.

"Nothing," Angelina responds, biting her lip like she's holding onto a secret.

We find Billy's dad in the backyard, sitting in a lounge chair sipping iced tea and reading *Golfer's World*.

"Hey, Dad," Billy calls as he opens the back door into the garden and holds it for Angelina and me.

Billy's dad lowers the magazine. "Hello there, Arie."

"Hi, Mr. Hernandez," I reply, glad to see him. Billy's dad always looks happy, ready with a smile and a joke, not like my dad, where every pained smile evolves into a grimace. Until recently.

"What are you kids up to today? And who's your new friend?" he inquires, nodding at Angelina who politely stands, hands folded, her right foot turned out.

"Angelina." Billy grabs her arm and pulls her forward. "This is my dad."

"Hello, Mr. Hernandez," Angelina replies. "Nice to meet you."

"It's nice to meet you, young lady," he replies.

"Can you help us drill holes in Arie's pearls?" Billy asks, all business-like.

"I'd be happy to. Billy has been telling me about your pearls," Mr. Hernandez replies. "I've been wanting to get a look at them." Tossing the magazine aside, he unfolds his long legs, rising from his seat, growing like a beanstalk. I glance at Billy, and think, not for the first time, how much he looks like his dad. Billy will be that tall one day.

"Let's go to my workshop," he suggests, leading the way.

We follow like a clutch of baby chicks. Billy's house resembles mine, only a little bigger. The workshop waits at the back of the house, a small room with a table and bench with various drills and bits hanging on a peg board on the wall above it and a cabinet full of little drawers holding all types of mysterious things.

Mr. Hernandez slides onto the bench and grabs the arm of a big magnifying glass attached to the wall and expertly swings it in front of his face. After positioning it, he turns on the built-in light. I've seen this routine dozens of times, but it always fascinates me. He makes magic in this room, conjuring bracelets and rings, hair clips and brooches from silver and gold, gems and beads, pounded and twisted into perfection.

"Let's see those pearls, Arie." Mr. Hernandez puts on his glasses and turns to me, his hand open, waiting.

I rummage open the pocket of my shorts and burrow deep, retrieving the pouch. I pull open the drawstring and gently pour the pearls into his hands. They cascade like an iridescent waterfall. He cradles my hoard easily into one huge hand, picking them one by one out of his palm and placing them on a white satin cloth spread on the work bench. Carefully, he studies them with the magnifier.

Solemnly, he looks up from his work. "Arie, where did you get these? They're rare and exquisite. I've never seen anything like them." He sounds a little suspicious.

Billy rushes to my rescue. "They were her mother's."

I can't help but wince a little at this fib, but I acknowledge the brilliance of it. A mention of my runaway mom always stops adults from asking awkward questions. If grown-ups find out someone has been mysteriously leaving gifts for me on the beach, they'll tell Dad—game over. He'd make me move to Indiana for sure. Mr. Hernandez glances from me to Billy, but says nothing, turning back to the pearls.

"Billy, get some water," he commands, intent on his task.

Billy pours water into a little trough and brings it to his dad, who settles it under a small vice grip made especially for pearls. Picking up the first pearl, he carefully locks it into place, while Angelina, Billy, and I hover around him, watching. After studying the drill bits, he picks one, inserts it into a small hand-held drill, lowers the vice and pearl into the trough, and begins the delicate business of creating a hole. "The water keeps the pearl from overheating and cracking," he informs Angelina and me. "The trick is getting the hole centered, especially on irregularly shaped pearls like these, though yours are rounder than most. On a regular pearl, this shape would be unacceptable, but on abalone pearls, it's part of their charm."

We watch in awe as he drills one pearl after another. Soon, they're all lined up on the cloth, ready to be buffed and strung.

"Billy, you can finish. Get the silk string, the good one, and let Arie pick out whatever clasp she wants, though the sterling silver will nicely set off the pearls. They deserve the best materials. If you use a silver bead between each pearl, it will add some length to the necklace and look nice. Arrange the pearls how I taught you, with the larger ones in the middle, the smaller ones tapering on each side to the clasp."

"Okay, Dad," Billy responds. "I remember how."

"Good. You kids have fun. Let me see it when you're finished. I'll be in the yard if you need any help." Mr. Hernandez stands up and ruffles my hair, Izzie fashion. For some reason I've never been able to fathom, adults can't seem to help messing with my hair.

"Thank you, Mr. Hernandez." I beam up at him.

"You're welcome, Arie. Enjoy the necklace but take good care of those pearls."

"I will, I promise."

Angelina and I rummage through the drawers filled with clasps while Billy fetches the silk and other tools and arranges them on the table like a surgeon's scalpels.

One of the clasps catches my eye—two hands holding a heart with a crown on it.

"Billy," I ask, taking the clasp to show him, "what about this one?"

"That's a Claddagh, an Irish symbol," he replies. "The hands symbolize friendship, the heart love, and the crown loyalty. Do you want that one?"

"Is it very expensive?" I ask, conscious of the big favor Billy's dad has granted me.

"It is one of the better ones," Billy acknowledges, "but Dad said for you to have what you want."

"Okay, then that's the one I want." I swallow the happy lump in my throat that threatens to bring tears of thanks. I can't wait to wear it.

Billy sets Angelina and me to work polishing the pearls while he attaches half of the clasp to one end of the strand of white silk he has carefully measured.

"This is French wire," he informs us. "It's coiled sterling silver, hollow like a tube, and slides over the thread." He cuts a tiny piece and pulls it through the needle and onto the thread. It bends to make a loop. See how I've used it to attach the clasp?"

Angelina and I admire his work.

"Angelina, can you bring that drawer of silver beads, the second one from front the left, the top row?" Billy gestures to the cabinet.

Angelina carefully slides out the drawer and carries it to Billy.

Then he begins laying the pearls out in a circle by size, just like his dad said, placing a bead between each one so I can see how it will look when it's finished. Though they're not round like regular pearls, to me they're the most perfect thing I've ever seen—each misshapen blob unique.

Then Billy shows us how to string the first pearl, knotting it securely in place and using a tiny drop of glue, followed by a silver bead.

"Do you want to string them all yourself?" Billy asks me.

"It will seem more special if you and Angelina help," I tell him. I string the next pearl as Billy and Angelina watch, Billy occasionally offering advice and helping to keep the thread tight.

"That's going to be one nice necklace," Angelina says. "Lucky girl, even if it is a little stalkerish."

I give her the stink-eye.

"Just kiddin'," she says.

When we're done stringing the pearls and beads, Billy attaches the other hand of the clasp and holds it up to the soft light streaming through the window. The necklace glitters, seeming almost alive in the sun, and streaks of shadows that play on its surface. It's more beautiful than I'd hoped.

"Let's see how it looks." Billy moves behind me and softly places the necklace around my neck, closing the clasp.

I reach up with one hand, feeling the weight of them, and then slide along their cool surface. They hang just right, the heavier ones in the center for balance, their abalone swirls of color reflecting in the silver of the beads.

"Wow," Angelina says in a hushed voice, "they're amazing!"

I move to the small mirror on the wall, Angelina and Billy following. A sudden memory breaks to the surface. I'm in Mom and Dad's room, sitting at her vanity. Mom stands behind, bending over me so she can see our reflection, her long dark hair brushing my face. I reach up behind me and grasp the strand of abalone pearls around her neck. Gently, she takes my hand, kisses it, then removes the pearls and places them around my neck.

I realize I'm crying.

"What's wrong, Arie?" Angelina asks. "Are you all right?"

"Did I do something wrong?" Billy's words collide with Angelina's.

I turn to Billy and put my arms around his neck. At first, he stiffens, but I don't let go. He relaxes into the hug, squeezing back, his face in my hair. The coppery odor of sweat and Ivory-soap smell of him, so familiar, balms my wounded spirit. "You did everything just right," I manage to say, letting go to hug Angelina. "Thank you," I utter, my voice still a little wobbly, "for helping."

Catching the glint of the pearls from the reflection in the mirror, I stare at myself, searching for more memories, though none come. I tuck this one into my mind to take out and examine later.

Chapter 12

I lie in bed, fingering the pearls, thinking of Mom. Sometimes I'm angry at her. Other times, I long for her to come back. Grasping the shard of memory of her and the pearls, my heart fills with love and hate, longing and loathing. Her sharp image consumes my inner world as her face comes into focus, clearer than ever. I do have her eyes. This realization shakes me wide awake. I thought she had loved me. Izzie says she still does, but I'm not so sure. If she loves me, she'd be here. She never would have left. Resentment shoves the longing and love out of the way.

Dad comes home tomorrow.

I miss him. And I'm afraid for him to come home.

What if he makes me move? The thought fills me with panic. My heart thumps like a rabbit, and I start to sweat. Tossing and turning, I punch my pillow into a lump, searching for coolness. Finally, I give up and kick the covers off, grab a sweatshirt and my phone, and quietly slip out in the hall past Izzie, sound asleep and lightly snoring, and tip-toe outside. I curl up in the hammock that Mom loved so much, where we had so many happy afternoons reading and napping. I text Billy, hoping he's awake but not expecting him to be.

Are you still awake?

Yes. Just finished my report.

His swift reply startles me. Our reports are due tomorrow, but I finished mine a week ago. Mrs. Krenwinkle pushed the due date to the last week of school. I usually look forward to summer, but now with Indiana looming in the future, part of me hopes it never comes.

Can't sleep so came outside to cool down.

My phone pings almost immediately:

Do you want me to come over?

I take a minute to respond. Billy's never come over at night except when we were little and had sleepovers. I feel a little funny about it but want to see him. Why not? I text back:*I don't want to get you in trouble.*

Don't worry about that.

Okay, if you're sure. I'm in the hammock.

I'll be right there.

While waiting for Billy, I look up at the moonlight filtering through the branches of the oak trees that anchor the hammock. The overcast day evaporated late in the afternoon; it's a clear night. I imagine Trevor with his telescope, examining the stars. Maybe he'll have news for us tomorrow. I'm trying to find the Little Dipper when I hear Billy quietly opening the gate, sneaking in like a fresh mist. When he reaches me, I shuffle over; he climbs in, squirming for position. He's slightly out of breath from running. We lie quiet for a while, Billy's hands behind his neck, and star gaze.

`"Is that the Little Dipper?" I whisper, pointing at a corner of the sky.

"I think so," he whispers back. "It looks like the North Star at the tip."

I snuzzle closer, and he puts an arm around my shoulders. I lay my head on his chest. It seems so natural, lying like this with Billy, calm and safe.

We talk softly, making plans for summer and surfing lessons, neither of us mentioning Indiana.

Eventually, the hammock lulls us to sleep.

***

"Wake-up!" I shake Billy, who startles up in alarm, nearly tossing us both out of the hammock.

"What's wrong?" he asks, looking around with owl-like eyes.

"It's almost dawn. You have to go home. You might get in trouble." I can tell by the sun that it's too late for the cove. "Just meet me at school."

"Right," he replies, untangling himself from the hammock and rolling out. He slips on his shoes, gives a silly salute, and slips out the gate as quietly as he came in. I hear the soft pad of his shoes as he takes off at a run and listen until he's gone.

Sneaking back into the house, I hear Izzie's almost-a-snore breathing, grateful that she's a sound sleeper. I ease into my bed and lie there until Izzie's kitchen noises assure me she's up. I get ready for school, my report secured in my backpack. Tucking the necklace under my shirt, I go to investigate the enticing aromas seeping into my room.

Izzie's making toast and fried eggs.

"Good morning, sunshine. Did you sleep well?" she asks.

I wonder if she knows and is trying to trap me. Attempting to appear innocent, I say, "I slept okay. Can I make an egg sandwich out of mine? I'm running a little late."

"Sure thing, Sugar Plum. You want tomato?"

"I'll get it." Ever since I read *Harriet the Spy* and discovered her quirky love of tomato sandwiches, I've had to have tomato on everything. I slice one, then the cheese, and take care of the toast. Izzie pours herself coffee while I pack up the sandwich and put orange juice in a small thermos.

"We'll probably go to cove after school," I tell her as I shoulder my backpack.

Overwhelmed by a sudden urge, I throw my arms around her waist and give her a tight squeeze.

"What's this all about?" she laughs.

"I love you, Izzie. I don't tell you enough."

"That's the truth. I love you, too, all the way to the moon." She hugs me back. "Get going so you're not late," she says, giving me a light push.

After class, we race to the cove, and I win by several yards. The tide's low, so we check Fisherman's Cove and then climb over the rocks to Shaw's. Trevor spots us and waves, smiling like a hyena, and runs to meet us.

"Hey, Sport," Billy greets him, "how have you been?"

"I went to Reese's house," he says, practically leaping out of his skin.

"Still in love?" I ask him.

"Yeah! We're going to get married when we're grown-ups," he informs us.

We try to suppress our mirth. Little kids are so cute.

"Guess what I saw last night?" Trevor asks.

We all look at him, serious now. "What did you see?" I ask, trying to be patient.

"Harry walking down the beach with the lady in the white dress," Trevor replies, triumphant.

"How do you know it was Harry?" Angelina questions him.

"The moon was full!" Trevor replies, indignant, turning to Angelina, hands on his hips, acting like she must not be very bright.

"Okay, kid," Angelina says, backing up a step with her two palms toward him. "I believe you."

"What time was that?" Billy interrogates him, his interest piqued.

"I'm not sure. I heard talking. It woke me up, so I went out on the balcony."

"Did you hear what they said?" I question, sensing something big is about to happen. It's unlikely he heard something way up there, but when the wind blows just right and the waves calm, it's possible.

"A little," Trevor replies, obviously enjoying all the attention. "Harry asked her, 'When are you going to tell her?' and she said, 'Soon.' But then they walked too far away for me to hear anything else. I watched from my telescope."

With questions in her eyes, Angelina leans over and whispers, "Do you think they were talking about you?"

"I don't know," I whisper back. "They could be, I guess." I want so much to believe Trevor's tale. What if it's my mom? Again I wonder if she's leaving the pearls.

I want to solve the mystery of the pearls, but I also don't want the magic to end.

"What does she look like?" I ask Trevor, trying to sound like it's no big deal.

"She has long dark hair, I think. I only saw her face through the telescope for a second. Did I do good?" Trevor asks.

"You did *really* good, kid," Billy tells him.

Angelina and I congratulate Trevor. His little freckled face glows with pride.

"Let's try to find Harry," Billy suggests. "I'll bring you something special tomorrow," he says to Trevor.

"Thanks, Billy!"

We leave Trevor happily digging in the sand and pick up our pace, determined to find Harry.

After searching Fisherman's Cove, Heisler Park, and the gazebo area, we finally find him huddled on a bench at Main Beach, hugging his knees to his chest.

I dig around in my backpack and find the squashed but edible ham sandwich, an apple, and a cookie I didn't eat at lunch.

"Hi, Harry," I say, handing him the food. "I'm sorry I don't have any coffee today."

"That's all right, Arie. Izzie came by earlier with coffee and soup. I'll tuck these away for later," he answers, shoving the food into a worn knapsack.

"We heard you have a friend," Billy ventures. "A pretty lady dressed in white."

Harry flashes suspicious eyes at Bill. "Who told you that?" he asks in his gruff-as-gravel voice.

"A friend of ours saw you walking on the beach with her last night," Billy replies, trying to sound nonchalant but failing.

"Your friend should mind his own business," Harry huffs, pulling a filthy blanket tighter around his shoulders, even though it's warm and sunny.

"Harry," I ask, trying to sound non-threatening, "who is the woman?"

"Yeah, why can't you tell us?" Angelina stands, her left foot crooked to the side, one arm on her hip, her no-nonsense stance.

"None of your bees-wax," he snaps, turning back to the ocean.

"You don't have to be mean," I tell him, annoyed by his tone. Sheesh. I'm just trying to find out who's leaving the pearls. "Does the woman in white live around here?" I ask, almost belligerent.

"She lives in the ocean," he says, shifting sly eyes toward me, gauging my reaction, I assume.

"That's impossible!" I cry.

"Impossible or not, it's the truth. Believe me or don't, it makes no difference. I'm just crazy ol' Harry, right?"

Billy stands right in front of Harry, forcing acknowledgement. "We mean no disrespect, sir. Honest, we don't. But we really need to know who the woman is. Can you please help us?"

Harry's eyes bore into Billy's, then seem to come to a decision. "I'll tell you this much: the woman is my friend, but if I told you about her you wouldn't believe me."

"But . . .." Billy tries to interrupt.

Harry cuts him off. "Listen. I've been living around these parts my entire life, and I know everyone. The woman belongs to the sea. She has secrets she's not ready to tell." His watery eyes reach out to mine. "Be patient, little miss. You'll find out everything you need to know. I've told you once before, August is the answer. Now you kids run along and let an old man be." That said, he stands, picks up his pack, and walks away toward the cliffs.

"But I may not be here in August," I say to no one in particular. Deflated, I hoist my backpack into a comfortable position, and turn to leave. Angelina and Billy quietly follow.

It seems my only hope is to try to talk Dad out of moving.

Billy and I walk Angelina home then go to my house. Dad's Prius is in the driveway.

Time to face the music, as Izzie likes to say.

"Do you want me to come in with you?" Billy politely inquires, but I can tell he doesn't really want to. I don't blame him.

"Thanks, Billy, but I better talk to him alone."

"Good luck, Arie. Text me later if you can," he says as he heads off at a brisk pace down the street.

Chapter 13

Standing on the porch facing the door, I take a deep breath, gathering my courage to face Dad. If I stay out here, it's safe. Inside the house, my world might shatter. It reminds me of Schrödinger's cat we learned about in science camp last year: a cat in a box with poison is both dead and alive until the box is opened; both possibilities exist. I'll either be forced to move to Bloomington or I won't. No more stalling. Time to see if the cat's alive.

Mouse-like, I slip in the door and gingerly set down my backpack, listening. Dad's whistling softly as he creaks open the oven door, releasing the delicious smell of Izzie's once-a-week famous almond-crusted salmon bake smothered in onions and parmesan.

"Ouch!" he yelps, as the dish clatters onto the stove top. The sound of running water tells me he's burned himself, trying to soothe it in the cool tap water.

Sauntering into the kitchen, I try to remain calm as if nothing has happened and pry an ice pack out of the freezer. "Hi, Dad. Looks like you've burned yourself again." Handing it to him, I advise, "Izzie says ice helps prevent blisters."

"Arie! Sweetheart, I didn't hear you come in." He tosses aside the ice pack and hugs me to him, making me feel awkward and on guard.

He steps back, retrieves the ice pack, and holds it on his hand, all smiles and happiness. Why is he so happy? It's so un-Dad like.

"How was your trip?" I try to sound casual but static tension crackles around the words like a mini electric storm. Dad doesn't seem to notice.

"Great!" he gushes. "Spring in Indiana—there's nothing like it. It's green and fresh with wide open spaces."

His sparkling eyes jab icicles into my heart.

"It's green and fresh here too," I point out, "all year long."

"Not like Indiana. You have to see it, Arie! I thought we'd take a little trip this summer, just the two of us, to see what you think." He tries to sound casual, but he's unsuccessful.

"I think I'll hate it." I sound like a brat and don't care. Is he trying to pretend I have a choice? How gullible does he think I am?

"Don't be like that, sweetheart," he wheedles. "We agreed not to fight. Let's eat this marvelous salmon Izzie baked."

He's not getting off that easy. "Dad, did you accept the job or not?" I block his way from the sink to the stove.

"Not yet." He stumbles over the words. "They're holding it for me until August." He steps around me and busies himself dishing salmon and rice onto two paper plates.

August? Harry keeps mentioning August. I wrack my brain trying to remember exactly what Harry said when he was babbling nonsense. Not knowing how to respond to Dad's comment, I retrieve the pitcher of sweet tea out of the fridge and put it on the table, along with two glasses.

We eat in silence for a while, though mostly I turn my food into mush, mashing it with my fork, the icicles in my heart having journeyed to my gut.

"When will you decide?" I finally ask.

"I have a couples of months yet," he mumbles, his mouth full of salmon and rice. He chatters on for a while about the glories of Indiana. I feel so sick I tune him out, but something he says grabs me by the ear.

"Marni says you'll love it there. She went to the private school I told you about."

His voice, bright and squeaky, sounds an alarm bell in my brain and freezes the forkful of salmon in midair. Calmly putting down my fork, I wipe my face with a napkin, and ask, "Who's Marni?"

"A friend I met at the San Diego conference last year," he remarks, trying to sound like it's not important, but his ears are turning red and he's avoiding my eyes. "She teaches cultural anthropology at the university in Indiana."

Does he have a girlfriend in Indiana? Is that what this is all about? It can't be! Dad's never gone on a date, not since Mom. At least I don't think so. But then I remember the postcard.

"Is *she* the reason you want to move?"

"Not entirely, no," he answers, sounding sincere. "There are other reasons, Arie, but I do like her, very much, and I think you'll like her, too."

My mouth hangs open like it's ready to catch flies. I clamp it shut, grinding my teeth in agitation. "What are the other reasons?"

"We'll discuss them another time," he says, sounding and looking uncomfortable, avoiding my eyes again and squirming in his seat, "when I think you're ready." He picks at his paper napkin like he does when he's nervous, tearing off tiny chunks, just like he's shredding my life.

"I'm ready *now*," I fume. "If you're going to ruin my life, you can at least tell me *why*!"

"Sweetheart," he says, using his I'm-the-adult-and-know-better tone, like Mrs. Krenwinkle. "I'm not ready to tell you. You wouldn't understand."

"Stop treating me like a baby!"

"Arie, I'll tell you when the time is right, and that's final."

His icepick voice chips open my anger, turning the ice in my gut to fire. What's happened to my sweet Dad? Why is he talking to me this way? It must be that woman's fault.

"Fine! But I'm not meeting your stupid girlfriend." I flounce out of the kitchen, grab my backpack and sweatshirt, and shout, "I'm going to Billy's" as I slam out the door.

I hasten on the sweatshirt, sling my backpack over one shoulder, and take off at a run, not stopping to text Billy. About halfway to his house, my feet, having lassoed my brain, abruptly halt. I don't feel like talking to anyone, not even Billy. Defiantly, I turn and head to the cove. Maybe Nessie will be there.

The sun is about to set, the sky a watercolor of crimson and blue. The tide's out, so I sit on the rocks, arms on my knees, watching the colors as they change to darker hues with the fading light, and search for Nessie. The thought of having to move away from the ocean's enchantment tears me in two. A part of me will die. I can't imagine a life without Billy, Angelina, and Izzie—and the magic of Nessie. I can't go. I won't. I'll run away first. I lay my head on my arms and cry big, shattering sobs.

"Everything will be all right, little lady," a gruff voice behind me says.

Scampering up, I abruptly swing around, facing the voice. "Harry! You scared me to death. I thought no one was here." Relief smooths my frazzled, pounding heart.

"I like to tuck myself into the rock face when the tide's out and enjoy the solitude. 'Whosoever is delighted in solitude is either a wild beast or a god.' Aristotle said that. Since I'm no god, I must be a wild beast."

"That's nice, Harry," I reply, dredging up a tiny smile.

"The sunset's a beauty tonight, isn't it?"

Despite its sandpaper quality, his voice oddly comforts my battered heart. "It is," I reply, wiping my face with my sleeve, slightly embarrassed, even if it is just crazy old Harry. I don't like people to see me cry.

"Everything *will* be all right," he tells me again. "You have my word on that."

"Thanks, Harry, but you can't help me. Dad's got a girlfriend and wants to ship me off to Indiana to be with her." I sit back down facing the ocean, and Harry sits beside me.

"How do you know I can't? You haven't given me a chance. I know I'm not right in the head, but I do know things." He stretches his legs out on the rocks, crossing them and leaning back on his elbows. "The craziness comes and goes. Right now, I'm as clear-headed as you," he says, sounding a little offended.

It can't hurt to humor him. And he does know the lady in white. "I'm sorry if I hurt your feelings. But how can you help?"

"For one thing, I can get a message to your mother," he says, matter-of-factly.

Glancing sideways at him, my voice dripping sarcasm, I ask, "How do you plan to do *that*?"

"Don't act so high and mighty, missy," he replies. "Do you want my help or not?"

"*Please*, tell me if the woman in white is my mom. You know who she is. If I can find Mom, maybe she can help."

He studies me carefully, his eyes cool and appraising. "I can't tell you that, but I do know how to get a message to your mom. You can believe me or not. Your choice," he says, and sniffs, turning back to the ocean.

I'm desperate enough to try just about anything. "Can you tell her about Dad trying to move me to Indiana?" Who knows? Maybe he really can help. I'm running out of options.

"Consider it done," he nods with certainty.

"How will I know if she gets the message?" I ask.

"You'll know. Just keep your eyes open. And keep this between the two of us, you hear? Your friends don't need to know for now," he replies.

"Okay, Harry. It'll be our secret. I better get home. It's getting dark. Dad might send out the armed forces." I try to sound funny but don't succeed.

Harry snorts at my lame attempt at humor. "Okay, you run along. I'll let your mom know what you said."

"Thanks, Harry." I pick up my pack, and wave goodbye, feeling a little lighter than when I got here. I don't think Harry really talks to Mom, but it feels right to tell a grown-up other than Izzie, though I have to think of a plan to trick him into telling me what he knows. I sigh. If being a grown-up means lying and keeping secrets from kids, I don't want to be one. Adults wonder why kids do the same thing. I think it's because we learned from them.

Walking in the cool night air helps clear my head. The porch light to the cottage shimmers in the slightly damp night air, guiding me home.

Dad's sitting on the steps.

"Arie." He stands, reaching out for me. "I've been so worried. I called Billy's house, and his dad said you never arrived. Where have you been? I was getting ready to call the police."

I take an involuntary step back. "That's ridiculous. I just went for a walk." I skirt past him and into the house, casually dropping my pack into a chair. He follows me in.

"You weren't down at the ocean, were you?" he says, his eyes full of panic.

"Why do you hate it so much?" I ask. "I love the ocean. I'm not going to drown, if that's what you are afraid of."

He runs his fingers through his hair, like always, when he's upset.

"Just stay out of that ocean, *please*. You don't understand! If you want to swim, go to a pool." He's almost shouting now.

"Then *tell* me *why!*" I yell back.

"Arie, I won't fight with you." He crosses his arms across his chest, trying to appear Dad-like, but unable to pull it off. He's always been my gentle, sad dad. Only now he's not so sad. *Marni* changed that. This realization stings me with resentment. Who is she, thinking she can ruin my life and steal my dad?

"Then don't make me move," I fling at him, while heading for my room.

"Arie, wait!" he pleads. "Nothing's settled yet. All I'm asking is that you give the idea a chance."

"Okay, Dad," I say, tired and sick at heart. "I just want to go to my room and read." But really, I don't want to talk to him anymore. I miss my old dad, even if he was a little sad.

"Okay, sweetheart," he relents. "I'll be in the living room if you want to watch TV with me. We can make popcorn and watch a movie," he offers.

"Maybe tomorrow." I walk away, feeling angry yet a little bit guilty, too, because I can't be happy for him.

Slumping dejectedly into my room, I dig my phone out of my backpack. The blue message light blinks. Eight texts from Billy. Too sad to be amused at his excessive worry, I text him back.

Hi Billy. I'm okay. I went for a walk.

Everyone was worried. You should have told someone.

I know. I just needed time alone. I'm sorry.

What did your dad say?

He has a girlfriend in Indiana. That's why he wants to move. There's another reason, but he won't tell me what. I think it's something about Mom.

A GIRLFRIEND?! Isn't he too old for a girlfriend? Grown-ups can be so dumb.

LOL. So true.

We chat for a while, but my heart's not in it. Finally, I tell him I have to go.

After brushing my teeth and putting on pajamas, I sit on the bed, feeling sorry for myself, the cool weight of the necklace against my skin. Izzie's philosophy of catching more flies with honey plays like an unwanted song in my head. Okay Izzie. You win. Listening to the TV sounds from the living room, I tuck my necklace secretively under my pajama top and join Dad.

He looks up from his show and smiles. Not saying a word, I sit next to him, curling up like a hedgehog against his softness. He puts his arm around me, pulling me close. A couple of rebellious tears escape, but I brush them away before Dad can notice. Using his free hand, he passes me the popcorn bowl. I munch on a handful but don't really want it. I just want my dad.

Chapter 14

A noise at my window wakes me in the dark. Three sharp taps followed by two quick ones. It's Billy's signal, his secret-agent knock from our little-kid days playing at being spies. I glance at the clock—4:00 AM. Rubbing the sleep from my eyes, I reluctantly crawl out of my warm nest, thumb back the old-fashioned lock, and lift the wooden-framed window.

Billy loosens the screen with his pocketknife—a trick we learned years ago—and pokes his silly head in, his hair rumpled from sleep.

"What are you doing here? It's 4:00!"

He ignores my cranky tone. Sometimes I think he knows me too well.

"I missed you." His half-clownish, half-serious smile tugs at my heart.

"Be quiet," I hiss. "What do you want?"

"I thought we'd get to the cove early, see if we can catch the mystery writer."

"Not a bad idea. I'll be right there." I push him back out the window, and he pretends to fall, exaggerating as if he's been shoved by The Incredible Hulk. I give him my don't-be-an-idiot face and fasten the screen into place.

We jog to the beach, our backpacks bumping and thumping a steady rhythm behind us. The deserted cove greets us with an eerie, iridescent light that signals morning approaching fast. The lifeguards aren't even here yet. They arrived with Memorial Day and will be here until after Labor Day, so I no longer worry about hiding my swimming. Izzie doesn't worry as long as they're here. Dad's another matter.

We sink down in the sand and wait for the sun, scanning the ocean for any sign of life.

"I can't see anything. It's too dark," Billy complains.

"You're the one who wanted to get here early, so stop whining. Look, see that shape moving near the rocks?" I point to a roundish silhouette bobbing up and down in the water.

Billy stands up, his eyes piercing through the ever-lightening morning.

"Do you think that's Nessie?" he asks, straining toward the water.

"I don't think so. It doesn't look like Nessie's head. The shape's all wrong. No snout." I stand up next to Billy, riveted by the movement in the sea as the shape slowly sinks under the surface, disappearing like a magician's trick. Speechless, we stand for a while, studying the water, hoping the creature reappears. As the light changes color with the rising sun, the rocks become sharper and more vivid, glistening slate-grey in its recently washed-by-the-waves brilliance.

"What do you think it was?" I ask, my voice shrouded by the wonder of this visitation from a mysterious being.

Billy takes my hand, curling his fingers around mine. Too awed by the magic of the morning, I don't question it but take a step closer to his side. He's never held my hand—not like this.

"I don't know," he replies, "maybe a dolphin?"

"It wasn't shaped like a dolphin. I didn't see a beak. Did you?"

"You're right," he nods, giving my hand a little squeeze.

I squeeze back.

"We'll probably never know." Billy's shoulders slump a little in disappointment. "Let's search for clues."

Hand in hand, we explore the beach, starting at the south end, and then circling around back to the spot by the rocks. The sun has fully risen, revealing our footsteps in the pristine sand. Morning-glories trail down the rocky slopes, a riot of purple entwined with the dull green of the spiky ice plants.

Billy abruptly stops. "Arie, look!"

Following the direction of his finger, I see it. Sand writing. Something looks different, though, the letters somehow not quite right. When we get close enough to make it out, my stomach does a somersault.

Don't worry

I let go of Billy's hand and step closer, thrilled at the familiar writing and the not-so-familiar words.

"That's weird," Billy says. "What do you think it means? Don't worry about what?"

"The only thing I'm worried about is Bloomington, Indiana, and Marni."

And leaving everything and everyone I love.

"It must be about that, but who's doing it? I haven't told anyone, have you?" Harry's serious face pops into my head like a hobo version of a jack-in-the-box. Did Harry talk to my mom? Is she leaving these messages? My heart beats so fast I can scarcely breathe.

"No, I swear. Who do you think it is?" Billy asks. "Any idea?"

"I…I don't know. Maybe it's Harry." As soon as I say it, I begin to doubt Harry and wonder if he's the one leaving the pearls and messages as part of his craziness. Logic tells me Harry would never be able to get such rare pearls. Could it really be Mom? Gazing at the letters, mesmerized by the comfort of the neat curly-ques, I beg for answers.

But none come. Only more questions.

"Are you okay, Arie?" Billy asks, retrieving my hand, his warmth melting my frozen fingers. "You look like you've just gotten off a roller coaster after eating too much cotton candy. And your hands are like snowballs." He takes both my hands in his, rubbing them with his own, stopping every few seconds to blow his warm breath on them.

"I'm fine. Just cold."

"Hey guys!" Angelina's shout rings across the sand, jolting me out of my worry. She bounds across the beach, exuberant as a puppy.

"What's got you all excited?" Billy asks, flashing his lazy, crooked smile.

"I found it!" she yells, waving a sheet of paper under my nose.

"What is that?" I ask, mystified by her enthusiasm.

"Your mom's handwriting," she replies, triumphant.

"Where did you get it?" I ask, reaching for it, skeptical.

Angelina hands the prize over, glowing with satisfaction. "Mom works in the federal building, the Ziggurat, in Laguna Niguel, in the records department. I watched over her shoulder the other night when she was working from home and stole her password. After she went to sleep, I snuck out of bed and looked it up on her laptop, then emailed it to myself and printed it out when Mom took me to the library last night."

"You're lucky she didn't catch you!" Billy exclaims.

"I waited until she was busy browsing the mystery section," Angelina explains. "A mad bull couldn't get her attention when she's caught up in her books."

While she and Billy chat, I excitedly read the paper. It's a copy of my birth certificate.

And there at the bottom is her signature.

Angelina and Billy crowd in, studying it with me. Glancing at the writing in the sand and then the signature, back and forth, several times, I finally say, "I give up! It's no use. They're similar but not the same. It could be anyone writing in the sand."

Billy reaches for the paper, and I hand it over. He lays it in the sand next to the writing, anchoring it with his flip-flops, then stands up, admiring his handiwork.

"When you stand back, they look more alike," Billy says, sounding confident.

"Maybe," I grumble, "but it's not an exact match."

"Of course not," he scoffs, "one's written in large letters in the sand and the other has small letters on a piece of paper. They're bound to be different. But they've got more similarities than differences." He bends down and points at the letters. The capital "D" in Delany and the "D" in Don't, are really close; both have that loopy figure eight at the bottom."

Angelina chimes in, "He's right, Arie. They're closer than they appear at first. And look at the "y" in both. They're almost an exact match!"

"The "n" in both also could be the same writer," Billy says.

I pick up my birth certificate and trace the letters in Mom's name with my finger, imagining her writing it, Kalysta Delany McGinnis. To hold something she had written dredges up all the mixed feelings—hurt, love, anger, all competing for first place. I keep my head bowed over the paper until I'm sure I won't cry.

"Maybe," I finally say. "Thanks, Angelina, for finding it. It means a lot to me." I carefully fold the paper and zip it into the pocket of my shorts. Changing to a lighter tone, I tell her, "You're becoming quite the little criminal—forgery, sneaking passwords, what's next? Armed robbery?"

Billy snickers, and Angelina punches me lightly on the arm. "It's only because you're such a bad influence," she counters.

On the way home, Angelina says, "Don't forget to get me a copy of your dad's signature so I can practice, Arie," Angelina reminds me.

"That's right! I'll give it to you tomorrow," I promise.

At home, I sneak in the house to play sleuth in Dad's office. I guess I'm the criminal now.

Chapter 15

On Thursday, the class pulsates with impatience at the thought of summer and freedom. Poor Mrs. Krenwinkle gives up trying to teach us anything and sends us out for recess.

When the final bell rings, Billy leads the way out the door ahead of the mob, using his height to carve a path through the sea of liberated students, Angelina and I close on his heels. Billy triumphantly tosses his backpack into the air and catches it. We agree to meet at my house and walk to the cove. Billy has chores and Angelina forgot her practice sheet of Dad's signature. She wants to see what we think.

When I get home, Izzie's in the back garden, clipping green beans off the stalk she named Jack because its tendrils are so long it looks like it's trying to climb into the clouds.

"Izzie, can we have supper on the beach so we can watch the sunset?" I ask, trying to sound innocent.

She gives me her I-know-you're-up-to-something stare, the one that used to immediately provoke a confession from me. This time, I stare her down. She laughs and tousles my hair like she always does. "I guess you're entitled to a few secrets at your age, but don't do anything foolish and be home before it gets completely dark."

"I will, I promise!"

"Humph," she replies. "You had better."

"What time is Dad coming home?"

"A little late, but he should be here by the time you return. Get the leftover chicken out of the fridge and I'll help you make the sandwiches."

We get into our sandwich-making rhythm, me gathering the ingredients and Izzie assembling them between slices of whole grain bread. I slice her creations—they always taste better when she makes them—into triangles and wrap them in Saran wrap.

"Did Dad tell you about *Marni*," I ask, drawing out her name like it's a bad word.

"Yes, he did," she scolds, "and you should be happy for him instead of giving him grief. He's been alone a long time. He deserves a life of his own, just as you do. Don't judge people before you meet them, Sugar Plum. It's mean-spirited."

"But—"

"But nothing. I know you're upset about Indiana, but that's no reason to be snarky. And you never know. Things might work out the way you want, but even if they don't, try to be kind."

"Sorry, Izzie," I say, humbled. "You're right. I'll be nicer."

"That's my girl. You might even like the woman if you give her a chance," Izzie offers.

"I doubt it, but I'll try," I grudgingly promise. How can I like someone who's ruining my world?

"There's a bowl of potato salad in the fridge," Izzie offers.

I retrieve the potato salad and grab small Tupperware bowls fill them with individual servings. We stow everything in a special bag that seals in the cold, and I sit on the porch, waiting for Billy and Angelina. Angelina arrives first.

"That was fast," I say.

"Mom dropped me at the corner on her way to the market. I have to be home by dark." "Me too. If not, Dad will call in the National Guard," I joke.

I hear Billy's skateboard before I see him. He hasn't ridden it in weeks.

"I got here as soon as I could," he says as he hops the curb, flips the board up, and catches it on its way down. He stashes it on the porch, grabs the heavy bag with our dinner, slings it over his shoulder, and opens the front gate. With a sweeping bow, he stands back and holds it open. "After you, ladies."

Angelina giggles and curtsies.

"Quit fooling around, you two. We're already late!" I complain. "Let's go."

"Whatever you say, Your Highness," Billy quips. "Let's race! On the count of three: one, two, three!"

Billy's such a clown sometimes.

We take off like racehorses. Billy has the lead, but our dinner slows him down. Angelina and I burn past him, and he struggles to regain his position, but he can't do it. When we reach the bottom of the hill, it's me first, then Angelina, and finally Billy, but only a couple of feet behind.

I'm going to have to train harder. He shouldn't be able to catch us carrying that heavy load.

We set up on the beach and gorge on chicken sandwiches while exchanging news.

Angelina pulls out the copy of the canceled check I'd sneaked out of Dad's office (he must be the only person left on the planet who writes checks instead of paying bills online), and then places it along with a sheet of her practice on the beach towel. Billy and I study her work.

"This last one's almost identical," Billy says. "You're really good."

"It's perfect!" I smile at her. Even the first attempts at the top of the page are good, though a little rough. But by the last few tries, she's nailed Dad's signature.

"Thanks." She shrugs like it's no big deal.

Billy pulls out the registration form for surf lessons and hands one to Angelina. "You better fill out Arie's so the writing matches the signature."

"Great idea." Angelina starts to work.

Billy's dad filled out his, and Angelina's mom signed hers.

"Did you bring the money?" Billy asks.

"Yep!" I rummage in my pack for the roll of bills I'd stashed away in an old pair of socks and hand them to Billy.

"Great! Dad wrote a check for mine, so we can use my money for Angelina. We have plenty!" He's so happy he's grinning like the Cheshire Cat.

We all are. Summer, here we come!

"I'll drop everything off tomorrow," he says. "I already talked to Jeff at Goff's surf shop. We can start next week!"

"Awesome!" Angelina and I say in unison.

"What about boards?" I ask.

"They provide them for the lessons, but I have mine and two of Dad's boards he said we could borrow for practice," Billy explains.

Billy has thought it all out. Despite having learned to surf from his dad, Billy promised to take lessons with me so I wouldn't be alone. He said he needed a brush-up course because his dad doesn't surf much now, but I think he's just being Billy—not wanting to be left out.

We pack up and climb the stairs, then walk along the sidewalk at the top of the cliff overlooking the ocean, searching for Harry.

"There he is!" Angelina points to the gazebo by the fancy restaurant, Las Brisas, Spanish for "the breezes."

With his elbows leaning on the railing, his chin in his hands, he gazes out at the sea, his profile sharp against the softness of the mist-covered water.

He looks so peaceful I hesitate. "Maybe we shouldn't disturb him."

"I don't think he'll mind, seeing as we have his dinner," Billy reminds me.

"Maybe you're right." I shake off the doubts. Harry probably is hungry.

We make our way to him, stopping a few yards away. Billy fakes a cough to alert him we're there, but he doesn't turn around.

"Harry?" Harry still doesn't respond, so I step a little closer.

"Keep your voices down," he commands in a soft hiss. "You'll scare her off."

Quietly moving closer, practically whispering, I ask, "Who're you talking about?" He's probably talking to a palm tree or something.

That's when I notice the squirrel perched on his shoulder, nibbling a crust of bread clenched between its tiny paws. I motion to Angelina and Billy to come closer and point at the dainty creature. It must be a baby. It's not much bigger than a baseball. We watch until it has finished its meal. Then it crawls down Harry's shoulder and disappears inside his jacket. Harry cups his hand beneath the lump nestled next to his ribs.

"Is that your pet?" Angelina asks.

"If she decides she wants to stay with me, then yes."

Concerned for the little critter, I question Harry, "Shouldn't it be with its mama?"

"Doesn't appear to have one. She might have been eaten by a coyote. That happens a lot around here," Harry says.

"It does? I've never heard that." I shudder. Nature, however grand, can be so cruel.

"Lots of coyotes 'round these parts. They'll eat anything. They especially like cats," he calmly explains. He must notice our horrified faces because he continues, "It's the way of the world, kiddos, and you might as well get used to it. If one thing doesn't devour you, another will."

Not knowing what to say to this bit of wisdom, I change the subject. "What's its name?"

"I call her Penia," he says, rocking the tiny bundle under his jacket.

"Puh-knee-uh," I repeat. "That's a funny name. Why did you name it that?"

"Penia is the Greek goddess of the poor. Don't they teach you little hoodlums anything in school these days?"

Harry sounds grouchy. But then he almost always does.

"How do you know it's a she?" Billy inquires, acting like he's caught Harry in a logic trap.

Harry simply responds, "I looked."

That silences Billy. You can't argue with that.

Taking the pack from Billy, I dig around until I find the sack for Harry.

Thank you kindly." He takes it from me and immediately opens it, tearing off a piece of bread crust, opening his jacket, and dangling it above. Two little paws reach out and snatch it.

"That's nice, Harry," I say, touched by his tenderness with the squirrel. "I'm glad you have a pet."

"Promise me something, little lady. If anything happens, you take care of Penia for me. She's not much trouble."

Trying to hide my astonishment at this request, I quickly answer, "Okay, Harry. But nothing's going to happen to you."

"Probably not," he says, his voice tinged with sadness, "but I like to keep my affairs in order just in case."

What affairs could he possibly have to put in order?

Putting his cap on, he nods at us and walks away without another word.

"Harry, wait!" I run to catch up with him. He doesn't stop, so I have to walk with him. I'm determined to get him to tell me if the lady in white is Mom. "You were right about Mom," I tell him. "I talked to her last night. She's not the lady in white."

"She is too!" he blurts without thinking.

"Thanks, Harry," I say. I can't believe my plan worked.

"You little rascal," he mutters. "What's the world comin' to when a snot-nosed kid plays a dirty trick on a poor ol' homeless man?"

"Sorry, Harry." I turn to leave. "Bye." He doesn't say another word, just quickens his pace.

"What was that all about?" Billy asks.

"Yeah," Angelina says, following Billy's lead.

I don't want to tell them until I'm sure it's her. I still have my doubts about Harry knowing anything about Mom. It could all be a delusion. "Nothing," I lie. "Just more Harry nonsense. Let's go before we miss the sunset."

We arrive just in time to watch it slip behind Catalina Island. The silver sky tinged with orange reminds me of a Cream-sickle, the kind we used to get from the ice cream shop when we were little. It's not as spectacular as some nights, but it will do. We gather up our gear and walk home. Billy and Angelina are elated at the thought of the long summer ahead.

I try to join in but mostly stay quiet, still wondering about Harry and Mom.

Dad's home when I get there. I hope we don't fight tonight.

I truck the empty dinner sack into the kitchen and begin to unload the leftovers and wash the Tupperware.

"Is that you, Arie?" Dad calls from his office.

"No. It's an axe murderer," I shout back.

He laughs, and with a scrape of his chair and lumbering gait, he's in the kitchen. My back is turned, still washing the dishes.

"Izzie told me you were picnicking at the beach with your friends. Did you have a good time?"

"Great!" I say, grabbing a dishtowel to dry my hands, chattering about our day. Dad's all smiles, but his expression shifts to something I can't quite identify. Anger? Hurt? Fear? A mix of all three?

Then I notice he's staring at my neck with anguished eyes.

My necklace! I forgot to tuck it in. I look down at it and back at Dad.

He takes two long strides and reaches me. Lifting the necklace, he runs his fingers through it. I hold my breath, waiting for the inquisition.

"Where did you get these pearls? Have you been going through my things?" His voice drips acid.

What does he mean, going through his things? "I haven't been 'going through your *things*,'" I shoot back, angry now and full of mockery. "These are mine." I'm outraged at his accusation, even though technically, I did go through his things a few days ago to get his signature.

"Don't take that tone with me, young lady!" he yells. "Where did you get them?"

Too shocked for words—Dad has never yelled at me, lectured, yes, but never yelled, at least not like that—I feel my eyes sting, betraying me by filling with tears.

Something in my expression must get to him because the anger quickly dissolves as he pulls me to him for a hug.

"I'm so sorry, Arie. I shouldn't have yelled at you. Please don't cry," he says.

I sniff back the tears and swallow hard, pulling away from him.

"Why are you so mad?" I ask.

"Just tell me where you got the necklace, okay? It's important." His eyes beg me not to question him, but I can't help it.

"First tell me why it makes you so upset," I say, "and then I'll tell you."

Defeated, he slumps down at the kitchen table, his head in his hands.

Alarmed now, I ask, "Dad, what's wrong? Are you all right?"

Raising his head, he runs his fingers through his hair and says in a deflated tone more troubling than his yelling, "Sit down, sweetheart. We need to talk."

I obey, waiting for him to make the next move.

"Your mother had a necklace just like that," he says as he reaches for it again, examining it closely, "but I can see now it's not hers. She didn't have these silver beads between the pearls."

Then my memory of her pearls is real, not just my imagination.

"I bought it for her when we first got married. She never took it off until the day she left. I couldn't bear to throw it out. I thought you'd found it."

He drops the necklace, which makes a solid thud against my chest.

I don't know what to say, so I sit and wait, fingering the necklace myself now, my heart racing.

"I'm sorry, honey. Seeing those pearls brought back a lot of painful memories. You look so much like her, and then when I saw the necklace . . .."

"Dad," I say, "why won't you talk about her?"

"You'll understand more about these things when you're older."

"How many times do I have to tell you I'm not a baby?" I literally bite my tongue, trying not to scream. "You always use that lame excuse. Just *tell me.*"

He sighs and looks down at me. "It hurts to think about her. I . . ." he swallows hard and gazes at the ceiling. "I don't want to lose you."

"Lose me? What are you talking about?"

"Arie, just drop it for now," he says, his voice cracking.

"It's not fair," I blubber.

Dad reaches out for a hug. "I know, sweetheart. I'm sorry. Give me some time."

"Give you time!" I push away. "Why is everyone always saying that to me?"

With a puzzled frown, he asks," Who else has said that to you?"

"Nobody." I turn to walk away.

"Where *did* you get them?" he asks, his voice more normal now. "The pearls, I mean."

"We found them. Billy and Angelina helped make the necklace, and Billy's dad let me have the silver beads and clasp." Strictly speaking, I'm not lying, just leaving out information.

"Found them?" he questions, sounding like he doesn't believe me for a second. "I find that highly unlikely. Where?"

Here we go again.

"At the beach by the rocks in Fisherman's Cove." Okay, that's a little bit of a lie, but still close to the truth. Besides, I'm beyond caring whether I have to lie to him. He's obviously keeping secrets from me. Two can play that game, Izzie always says.

"All at once? A pile of pearls like this is worth some money."

"No, they washed up on the shore. It took a few weeks to find them all." Again, it's not entirely a lie. Okay, so maybe I care just a little.

"Are you sure someone didn't give them to you?"

"Who would give me pearls?" I scoff, trying hard to convince him, but I'm squirming with uneasiness. I can't let him find out about the mystery writer.

"I thought maybe . . . well, never mind. They're very beautiful," he says, neatly changing the subject.

Relieved at the reprieve, I jabber on about the pearls, how I found them, embellishing as I weave a credible version, staying as close to the truth as possible without giving away the mystery writer.

Finally, at a loss for anything else to say, I suggest, "Let's watch a movie."

"Good idea," he says, glad to get away from the subject of pearls and back to something like our old routine, before Indiana and Marni. "I'll get the ice cream," he offers.

"I'll get my pajamas on and find a show." At least now I can wear the pearls without having to hide them.

We spend the evening eating ice cream and watching TV. I fall asleep while Dad's watching one of his cop shows but wake up later in my bed.

Chapter 16

On Monday, Angelina, Billy, and I take the Laguna Beach free trolley to Thalia Street Beach, three miles south, arriving early, antsy, as Izzie would say, to get started. Thalia is one of the more popular surf spots, but we rarely go there because it's so far.

Thalia, similar to Diver's Cove, with its houses staggered above on the cliffs, dozes in the morning light filtering through the haze, promising a beautiful day once it struggles through the overcast.

Billy arranged everything with Jeff from the local surf-and-tours shop. Surfing is all we talked about over the weekend.

At 9:00, Billy spots him, a twenty-something looking guy with shoulder-length blond hair and clear, hazel eyes. He strides easily across the sand, wearing swim trunks and a white t-shirt with Goff's Tours stenciled boldly across the front in blue lettering. Slung across his shoulder hangs a huge canvas bag, and he carries a surfboard under one arm.

"Hi, Billy," he says while anchoring the board upright in the sand and depositing the bag next to it with a cheery, drawn out, "Hello, *ladies*," causing Angelina and me to reply with a silly giggle.

"Who wants to fetch the other boards out of my truck?"

"I will!" Billy races across the sand and up the steep steps to the jeep parked at the top of the street.

Jeff introduces himself. "Let's see what size wetsuits you girls need." He rummages around in the bag, pulling out a few wetsuits in various sizes.

"Which one of you is Angelina?"

"Me!" Angelina pipes up, excitement oozing from every pore.

"Then you must be Arie," he says, his perfect smile flashing in his bronze-tanned face. He holds wetsuits up to us until he finds the right fit and hands us each one. Billy huffs up, lugging two more surfboards. He and Jeff prop the boards next to the other one where they stand in a circle like a modern-day, mini Stonehenge. Last year, I discovered a book in Dad's office filled with pictures of standing stones in England and Scotland. Stonehenge loomed off the page, full of magic and mystery.

I'm going to travel there some day when I'm grown up.

"I brought my own wetsuit," Billy offers, pulling it out of his backpack.

We struggle into the suits, trying to avoid getting sand inside. Billy finishes first, then helps Angelina and me tug hers on.

"These are our smallest boards, six feet, called soft tops or foam boards," Jeff informs us, "about the right size for you girls to learn on and softer in case of an accident. When you're more experienced, you can graduate to ten footers."

From most adults, it would seem like a boring lecture, but Angelina and I listen to Jeff, spellbound. Even Billy, who knows Jeff, pays attention.

I glance over at Billy.

He looks so grown-up, different somehow, his hair longer. A dark brown lock curls in the middle of his forehead, drawing attention to his straight nose and perfect mouth. I never thought of him as cute before.

Stop thinking like a stupid girl. Pay attention.

"Most beginners don't understand if you start too small, below six feet, you'll struggle more and have trouble transitioning to the longer boards," he continues. "Billy, you take the seven-footer since you have some experience."

First, Jeff has us each pick up our boards to get used to their weight, then tells us to place them in the sand like we're putting them in the water. We lie belly down on our boards and practice-paddle, flailing our arms and legs, Jeff correcting our form.

Billy makes faces at us, sucking in his cheeks to shape his lips and move them fish-fashion. He's such a goofball. I bite my lip to keep from snickering.

Then we practice hopping up from the paddling position. Jeff goes through all the moves: how to balance with our arms, position our feet and legs, how to bend our knees, and finally, how to step forward or backward on the board while maintaining balance.

Jeff talks about the waves, how to watch for the size of the swell to determine when to stand up and go for it, gesturing at the undulating ocean as he lectures.

"Okay, time to hit the water!" Jeff takes a baseball-pitcher's stance, cocks back his arm, and throws an imaginary baseball into the waves.

I can almost hear it smack the ocean's surface.

We wade out, then climb on and paddle, but Jeff halts us before we get too far.

"Let's practice in the smaller swells before we try deeper water," Jeff says. "Arie, you first."

Jeff holds on to the side of my board while Angelina and Billy straddle theirs and watch.

Billy frowns at Jeff. Could he be jealous? The thought gives me a little thrill. I smile at Jeff. He smiles back. I glance over at Billy. He doesn't look happy.

"Okay, Arie, practice hopping up like I showed you in the sand. And don't worry, I've gotcha."

"I'm not worried," I respond, excited to finally be standing on a board in the ocean. I hop to a standing position and try to balance, but instead, fall off and hit the water hard. When I emerge, Angelina and Billy are laughing.

I'm happier than I've been in a long time.

On the fifth try, I make it, a little wobbly, but still on the board. After a few more tries, Jeff lets me practice alone while he helps Angelina. Billy manages it without a hitch, as balanced as a boxer, his footwork perfect.

Once Jeff has decided we can all handle our boards, he illustrates how to catch a wave, calling out instructions as Angelina and I clumsily try to keep our balance.

I'm all lined up, waiting for the "go" signal, while Billy and Angelina wait their turns. Finally, Jeff shouts, "Now, Arie!"

I catch the wave, then scramble up, maneuvering into position.

I'm surfing! I can't believe it!

Salt spray stings my face as I balance precariously on the board, savoring every second. Then I miss a beat and fall back, my arms going like windmills as I try to regain my balance. I fall off, but I love every minute.

. "You're a natural," Jeff says, smiling and giving me a high five when I walk out of the water, dragging the board by its leash.

While Jeff goes to his backpack for water, instructing us to do the same, I say to Angelina, loud enough for Billy to hear, "Jeff's cute!"

"He sure is!" Angelina stares dreamily at him.

Billy glares at me. Maybe he really *is* jealous.

It's my turn to watch Angelina. She falls a few times, but finally catches a wave while on her knees hanging onto the sides of the board, riding in looking as happy as I feel.

Billy goes next. Of course, he kills it the first time and can't resist some fancy footwork, walking along the board like a pro. But he was lucky enough to have his dad teach him when he was little.

"Show off!" I yell. Billy sticks his tongue out and glides in.

Our time's almost up, so we all go out together, taking turns catching the waves, Angelina and I falling off a lot. When we're finished, we help Jeff stow the gear in his truck.

"You kids did great!" Jeff tells us. "Keep practicing but take it easy, and don't surf without a lifeguard nearby."

We wave goodbye and grab our backpacks.

Chapter 17

Every day we practice as much as we can, catching the summer trolley, stashing our boards in the back window like we've seen other kids do. We get off at the top of Thalia Street, feeling like pros, strutting down the quiet lane with Billy's dad's boards tucked snugly at our sides. Billy's wood-grained ride gleams from the sheen of wax lovingly applied. It's a beauty, the blond wood contrasting with the darker swirls patterned through it, the edges a deep mahogany—a work of art.

Angelina chose the scenic one, a dark maroon patterned with three dolphins in mid-leap above the waves, reminding me of the 17th century woodcuts of owls and other animals by Conrad Gesner that Dad loves so much.

Mine's a study in blue stripes, almost navy along the outer edges, gradually softening to the paleness of a robin's-egg blue at the center. I love it. But I wouldn't care if it were the ugliest board on the beach—as long as I can surf.

Sitting on our boards in the yogi pose like Zen masters, facing the beach, we rock with the gentle rhythm of the ocean, gazing at the sun peeking out from behind the hills of Laguna Beach. The silence, the aroma of salt and seaweed—it's the most peaceful feeling in the world.

As the sun heats up, so does the surf, and I find myself struggling to keep my balance. Angelina decides reading would be more reasonable and returns to our spot to lounge under the beach umbrella, absorbed in *The House on March Lane*, another girl detective novel.

If she doesn't become a famous sleuth or spy, I'll be very surprised.

"Maybe we should go in, too." Billy scans the rising surf.

I glance over at him straddling his board as we wait for the next swell, one eye closed from the harsh sun as he studies the big waves setting up outside the break point.

"You go ahead. I'm gonna ride some more." I get up on my knees.

"That's not a good idea, Arie."

"Are you *chicken*?" My dare, which usually gets him to do whatever I want, earns me an exasperated look.

I dismiss him with a wave toward shore. "Just a couple of more. I'll be right there."

He shakes his head. "Suit yourself."

I ride two more exhilarating waves and line up for a third. I'll go in right after this one.

Then I look up and see a towering wave barreling toward me. I'll never catch it in time. It's too fast!

Trying not to panic, I shove off my board to get clear of it and try to dive under before the wave breaks, just like Jeff taught me, but I'm too late. It slams me hard, knocking the air out of my lungs and snapping my leash. I can't tell whether I'm up or down as the water and sand angrily swirl around me, finally pounding me to the ocean floor.

Survival mode kicks in as I struggle to right myself, get my bearings and launch to the surface, but it's no use. The roar of another wave crashes above, wreaking more havoc and confusion.

A strange voice reaches out through the chaos and into my head, like Nessie.

But it's not Nessie.

"You can hold your breath a long time," it reminds me. "It's okay. I won't let anything happen to you." A silken dark body slides beneath and pushes hard, relentless, directing me, and I obey, the voice soothing my panic. Finally, we reach calmer water.

Rising to the surface, I take a deep, cleansing breath, not so much because I need air, but just to reassure myself. I search about, trying to find the source of the voice, and spot an unfamiliar seal swiftly making its getaway. It's a darker seal with beautiful white spots mottling its coat.

"Thank you!" I shout. It briefly turns, nods, and dives. That's so weird, but I'm getting used to strange happenings.

When I look toward shore, I see a lifeguard with her red life preserver swimming like a shark's after her, heading straight to me.

"Are you all right?" the lifeguard asks as she reaches me.

"Um…sure, I'm fine." How am I going to explain this?

"How did you get out this far so fast?" She's looking at me like I've grown a second head.

"I just, well, I swam hard to get out of the waves." That sounds phony, even to me.

"Let's get you to shore. Do you need the life preserver?" the lifeguard asks.

I don't, but since she swam all the way out here after me, it's the least I can do. She can play the hero. "Okay," I nod.

"Okay, then let's go." She expertly slips the belt over my head and under my shoulder. I relax as she puts her arm across my chest and tows me in, while I lie on my back, kicking a little to help.

It's a little silly, all this fuss. I could probably beat her to the beach if I wanted to.

Angelina and Billy are pacing the shoreline, Angelina peering under her hand, trying to see through the sun glinting off the water.

The rough ocean still tries to batter us as we near the sand, but the lifeguard brilliantly maneuvers us through the foam.

"Arie! You scared us to death!" Angelina's face is a cross between anger and relief. "Why didn't you come in with Billy?"

"If I'd known that wave was out to get me, I would've." My sense of humor doesn't amuse her. She puts one hand on her hip and glares at me. Billy gives me that I-told-you-so smug face.

"Where's my board?" I ask, scanning the sand, spying it a few feet away. Waves must have pushed it to the sand, and I see drag marks where someone hauled it out of the way of the waves. "Thanks!" I shout to no one in particular as I grab the board's leash and pull it to where Billy, Angelina, and the lifeguard stand watching me.

"You kids be careful. Stay out of that water until it calms down." The lifeguard's eyes catch mine, and she looks like she's about to say something, but then turns and walks away.

I can't help but exhale in relief. I hadn't realized I was holding my breath. Now I only have Billy and Angelina to deal with. Maybe I'd better just tell them the truth so they stop worrying.

They stand Superman style, demanding attention.

"I'm really sorry, guys," I begin.

"Sorry doesn't cut it, Arie. You need to tell us what's going on." I haven't seen Billy this upset since fourth grade when a big dumb sixth grader knocked him off the swing at recess.

"I know. I'll explain as best I can. Let me get dried off."

Billy tosses me a towel but remains standing.

I collapse on the blanket under the umbrella, and make room for them, motioning for them to join me. Reluctantly, they do. We sit in a circle, guru style. I scooch as close to them as I can get so we won't be overhead.

"When the wave smashed me, I heard a voice tell me it was okay. And then I felt a seal pushing me up from the bottom of the ocean and out to sea. I thought at first it was Nessie, but it wasn't. This seal had spots."

"A harbor seal," Billy automatically says.

"What do you mean, you *heard a voice*?" Angelina studies my face, trying to use her detective skills to see if I'm lying.

"I can't explain it." I raise my hands to my side, palms up, hoping to make them understand. I rush on. "Sometimes I hear a voice when I'm with Nessie, like she's talking to me, but it's in my head. But then I heard this other seal, too. I don't know how or why, I just can."

"You mean, like telepathy?" Billy's eyebrows widen until they almost collide with his hairline.

"Yeah, like that." Suddenly, I'm dying of thirst. Brushing the hair out of my eyes, I reach in my backpack for a bottle of water and gulp down half.

Billy and Angelina exchange worried glances.

"Do you think she has what Harry and your uncle have?" Angelina asks Billy, as if I'm not there.

"I don't think so. She's too young. Dad says it usually begins around seventeen or eighteen."

"Will you two stop talking about me like I'm invisible?" I yank at my bag and shove the bottle back in and zip it up, tugging so hard it gets stuck. Irked, I toss the bag behind me.

"You have to admit your story sounds crazy, Arie."

I hate when Billy uses that reasonable tone, like I'm a three-year-old.

"Why do you think I haven't told you?" My haughty look doesn't even faze him. "Now I'm sorry I did!"

"But hearing seals in your head doesn't explain your sudden aqua-woman powers."

Angelina has a good point.

"Yeah, what about that?" Billy cocks his head at me.

"If you think it sounds crazy that I hear seals talk, you'll haul me off to that hospital your uncle's in when I tell you."

Billy has the grace to look uncomfortable. "Okay, I promise not to call the doctors if you tell us how you're staying under so long."

"I promise, too." Angelina puts her right hand over her heart for emphasis.

They look sincere, so I plunge ahead. "I don't know that I can explain it, exactly. But when I'm with Nessie I can do impossible things. And now it's the same with this new seal. It's not that I'm holding my breath. I just don't need to breathe. And I see everything so much more clearly in the water than I used to. My eyes don't sting from the salt. I swim faster and longer without even trying, like I belong in the ocean. I don't know what's happening to me, but it's *wonderful.*"

"Maybe you should see a doctor, Arie, just for a check-up I mean, not the mental doctors," Angelina suggests, her eyes pleading with me not to get mad.

"But I feel great! *Really* great. Better than I ever have."

"Maybe we should test you." Billy's got his scheming face on.

Suspicious, I ask, "What kind of tests?"

"Just timing you underwater, stuff like that," he says, as if it should be obvious, "to see how long you can hold your breath."

"Good idea! And I can get my mom's blood pressure cuff." Angelina looks excited at the idea of playing nurse. "And a thermometer. We'll want to take your temperature, too."

"If that makes the two of you feel better, then okay." They're not going to let up so I might as well go along with it.

Later, on the way home, Angelina and Billy chatter away, making plans for turning me into a human guinea pig.

We say goodbye at my fence, and I open the gate to see Dad stepping out of the door, like he's been waiting for me.

"I need to talk to you, Arie."

Chapter 18

Dad ushers me into the house.

Casually tossing my backpack onto the wicker chair next to the door, I face him, trying to act like I don't suspect anything, but his expectant expression tells me otherwise. "What's up, Dad?"

Something big is happening. He's excited but nervous. I see it in the way he can't keep still. I follow him in, attempting to hide the distress threatening to rise to the surface.

"Don't' worry. I didn't cook." His attempted joke fizzles out like flat soda.

"Izzie left a pasta salad and a pitcher of lemonade," he informs me, his voice a little shaky now.

I force a smile and imagine myself looking like a demented hyena.

A white tablecloth patterned in purple irises covers the table, a delicate lavender vase with fresh wisteria gracing the middle. Two of the better dishes, the white ones with the scalloped edges that Izzie refers to as our Sunday best, balance out the scene. Dad's even folded cloth napkins around the silverware. A ghost of a memory shimmers at the edges of my mind. Mom places a birthday cake topped with five purple candles in the middle of the table.

My fifth birthday—and the last one with Mom.

"What's all this, Dad?" I wonder what he's up to. Whatever it is, it can't be good.

"I haven't seen you much lately. I want to have some time with my little girl." Affectionately, he ruffles my hair.

His soft grey eyes and shy smile don't do much to reassure me.

"It looks pretty." My efforts to sound enthused ring hollow; I'm simply waiting for whatever bad news he's buttering me up for.

He's so full of surprises lately and not the good kind.

While he pours the lemonade, I retrieve the salad from the fridge and place it on the table. Dishing pasta onto his plate, he asks, "What have you been doing all day?"

I lower my eyes so he can't see my face. "Just hanging out with Billy and Angelina." I don't know how to talk to him anymore. It used to be so easy. "What about you?"

I think he realizes it's a distraction ploy, but he goes along with it anyway.

"I'm researching the legends of several tribes of the Amazon. I'm planning to write a book. There's so little known about these cultures. Some of them have remained hidden from civilization for centuries."

As he chatters about his favorite subject—myths and legends—I study him. He has that happy glint in his eye, the one I've only seen since he returned from Indiana. Marni smarmy eyes. "That sounds cool, Dad. Will you read some to me?" Another distraction, which doesn't fool either of us. I haven't asked him to read to me in years.

We're getting better at going along with each's others keep-the-peace phoniness.

"I'd like that." He turns his attention back to his dinner.

We eat in silence, enjoying the mix of fresh peas and basil, made-by-hand pasta noodles and shrimp coated in Greek dressing. I stab at Kalamata olives and pieces of feta cheese, trying to maneuver them into my mouth along with a piece of pasta before it all falls off the fork.

"I need to tell you something, sweetie." Carefully placing his fork on his plate and patting his mouth with his napkin, he finally comes out with it. "I hope you'll not be upset. I've invited Marni to visit. She arrives this weekend."

I should have known. I stare into my plate, hands folded in my lap, fighting back the tears. Izzie's voice plays in my head. "Don't judge people before you know them. It's mean-spirited."

I take a sip of lemonade, fumbling for something nice to say. "That's good, Dad." A stray piece of lemon pulp catches in my throat. I cough to clear it and take another sip.

His beaming smile kills me.

"How long is she staying?"

"A few days, over the 4th of July."

Swallowing hard, I try to sound normal. "Where will she stay?" His pained expression tells me he doesn't want to talk about it, but with my pointed stare shooting darts into his brain, he has to answer.

"Uh . . . well, she'll stay at a hotel in town."

"She's not staying here?"

He looks a little shocked at this question.

"No, of course not," he stammers. "But I'd like to have her here for dinner, let you two get to know each other. And maybe we can walk to the beach together for fireworks."

I don't like this, not at all.

But I respond, "Okay, Dad, if that's what you want." As I say this, my brain tries to plot out some sneaky revenge on Marni, but Izzie's stern face blocks the thought. Instead, I take my frustration out on the salad, stabbing harder than necessary at an olive trying to escape its doom.

In an uneasy silence, we both poke at our food, taking small bites, chewing thoughtfully. After a few minutes, I blurt out, "I hope you're not cooking. You'll scare her off for good."

He almost chokes on a mouthful of pasta, coughs, takes a gulp of lemonade, but laughs so hard the lemonade squirts out of his nose, sending me into hysterics and him into a coughing, snorting fit.

After regaining his composure, he smiles a full-toothed grin, something I've *never* seen, and says, "No, smarty-pants. I'll get take-out."

"P.F. Chang's?" I love their Kung-Pao Shrimp. Next to Izzie's cooking, they're the best.

"That's a little fancy, don't you think?" His eyes twinkle.

"You're trying to impress a girl, so no, it's not too fancy."

"Okay, you little schemer. I can't argue with that. P.F. Chang's it is."

He looks so happy it hurts my heart. But part of me loves this cheerful Dad. If only he didn't want to move to Indiana, I could accept Marni. At least I think so. To be honest, I don't like the idea of sharing Dad with anyone. But as Izzie pointed out, he deserves to have a lady in his life.

I help Dad clean up, and then we watch *Dancing with the Stars*. It's one show we agree on, though I think it should be named *Dancing with the Nobodies*. The so-called stars are mostly people I've never heard of. But we like discussing the dancers, casting our votes, and then comparing our scores with the judges.

After the house quiets down and Dad's asleep, I text Billy.

Are you still awake?

He swiftly replies, and I picture his long, familiar fingers flying over the keys

I'm playing video games on the computer. What's up?

Marni's coming to visit this weekend.

Your dad's girlfriend? Awkward.

Yeah. I'll have to try to be nice. I realize my face is crunched into a grimace so I try to relax it.

Maybe, if she likes you, she'll move here instead.

I hadn't thought of that. He has a point.

It's worth a try, I text back, trying not to get my hopes up.

Want to go to the beach and talk about it?

Now?!

Billy loves to sneak out, but it's risky. We'd both be grounded for the summer.

Why not? Nobody will know.

He's probably right. Dad sleeps like a corpse. One time I put a mirror under his nose to see if he was breathing.

Okay, let's do it!

I'll be right there!

Excited at the idea of pulling one over on Dad, I tiptoe around my room, slip on my shorts and a sweatshirt, then roll up a spare blanket to make a reasonable imitation of a kid under the covers. I slide the window open, pry off the screen, toss out my Vans, and sit on the windowsill to wait for Billy. When his form takes shape under the streetlight, I hop down, slowly replace the screen, and join him. I hold onto his arm while I slip on my shoes. We don't say a word until we turn the corner.

"Let's run." Billy takes my hand and sets off at a slow jog.

I run beside him, enjoying the delicious thrill of the night and his warm hand in mine. We slow at PCH, ducking behind a fence to wait for a sleek black Mercedes to whiz by.

"The coast is clear," Billy whispers, and we race across, quiet as cats, and down the steps to Fisherman's Cove.

Drenched in moonlight, the cove glistens like something out of a fairy tale. A ribbon of light shines across the calm water like a pathway to the under-the-sea kingdom, that magical realm I'm just getting to know. I look for Nessie, but the water is still except for a few gentle ripples stirred by the outgoing tide.

We climb the rocky shelf and settle our backs against its solid bulk, reassuring me that some things, at least, are permanent.

Billy sits with his long arms casually draped across his bent knees. "So," he begins, "tell me about Marni."

"I don't know much, but Dad wants me to have dinner with them and watch fireworks."

"That doesn't sound so bad. And I'll be there with my mom and dad, like always. And maybe Angelina can come, too, so you can pretend you accidentally run into us." He sits there, smiling at his own cleverness.

"That would be great!" I'm so lucky to have such good friends. "Now I just need a plan to win her over."

"We can talk it over with Angelina tomorrow," Billy says.

"Do you really think I can convince her to move here?"

"I don't see why not. Who could resist you?" His voice sounds serious, not mocking, with a tinge of wistfulness at the end.

I study his profile, puzzling over what he could be thinking, as he stares out at the sea.

Suddenly, he turns, leans in, and brushes his lips lightly on mine.

I pull back in surprise. He just looks at me with those dark eyes.

I look back.

He picks up my hand, and I let him.

We sit there, thrilled and content, not needing words. It's always been Billy and me. And always will be.

Billy, sounding reluctant, finally breaks the spell of silence. "We should see if we can find Trevor and Harry tomorrow. Maybe they have some news."

His abrupt change of subject makes me smile. He's right. We've been so wrapped up in surfing we haven't visited our usual spots.

"Good idea. We can go to the cove early and wait for Nessie," I suggest.

"Sounds like a plan." He jumps up and stretches out his hand to help me up (not that I need it, but he's like his dad, a gentleman, as Izzie would say), so I don't protest like I did when we were little kids, determined to do everything Billy did but even better—and by myself.

We slowly walk home, holding hands, not talking much.

Then Billy says with a frown, "I didn't like it when you were flirting with Jeff."

I knew he was jealous! I say, "I wasn't flirting!"

"Yes, you were." He puts his arm around me, and I lean into him.

We stay that way, slowly walking home, loving each second.

When we get to my window, Billy takes off the screen. We stand there, face to face, and Billy puts his hands on my shoulders, kisses me again, whisper-light, then helps boost me through the window and replace the screen.

He waves as he jogs down the street. I stand at the window, two fingers on my lips, and watch until he disappears into the night.

Chapter 19

The smooth, comfortable rhythm of Dad and Izzie's voices wakes me. Dad's up early.

I shower, slip my bathing suit on under my clothes, and shove a towel, sunscreen, an extra shirt, and a few other things into my backpack.

As I rush into the kitchen, I grab an apple from the fruit bowl, kiss Dad on the cheek, and say, "Hi, Izzie! Can I have my breakfast to go? I'm late meeting Billy."

Crunching a juicy bit of apple, I notice Izzie's quizzical face. She glances at Dad, whose face resembles a startled owl.

"You're in a good mood today," he ventures, smiling with a hint of apprehension, maybe even suspicion.

"Can't a girl be happy?" I hug him around the neck, squeezing hard, take the two egg sandwiches Izzie has popped into a paper sack, hug her too, and bounce out of the house. Billy is waiting by the gate with a stopwatch.

Oh, yeah. I guess it's my day to play guinea pig.

"You're late." He tries to sound like he's irritated, but his ear-to-ear smile tells me he's happy, too.

"That's because *somebody* kept me out late last night!" I toss my hair, a trick I've only recently discovered since I've not cut my hair in a while. It's always been so short there's been nothing to toss. But I kind of like it longer.

I thought I'd be nervous or shy seeing Billy after the kiss last night (I still can't believe it happened), but I'm not. He doesn't seem to be, either. Somehow, it feels right, like we've always belonged together. We're simply changing. In a nice way.

As soon as we're out of sight of my house, I entwine Billy's fingers in mine.

"I texted Angelina last night." He casually swings my hand as we head down the hill at a quick pace. "She'll be a little late."

After scanning the beach for Nessie or messages in the sand with no luck, we sit on a rock and devour our sandwiches.

"Hi guys!" As Angelina runs through the sand, something odd hangs bouncing around her neck.

When she gets closer, I make it out. A stethoscope.

Let the fun begin.

"A stethoscope! Cool. Can I see it?" Angelina pulls it from her neck and hands it to Billy.

He carefully places it in his ears like it's the Holy Grail or something and listens to his heart.

"I have a blood pressure cuff, too." Angelina rummages in her backpack and triumphantly pulls out another instrument of torture.

"Where did you get this stuff?" I ask.

"Mom has high blood pressure, and she bought the stethoscope for me at a yard sale when I said I wanted to be a doctor. Now that I want to be a detective or secret agent, it's been stuffed in a box in my closet with a lot of other junk I outgrew."

Billy tries to stick the stethoscope to my chest.

I step back.

He steps forward.

I step back again, suddenly shy.

"Okay, if you won't let *me*, then Angelina can do it." His eyes gleam and his mouth mischievously turns up at the corners as he hands the scope back to Angelina.

She cautiously approaches, gingerly holding the end of the instrument toward me like I'm an angry cat with its claws out. When I don't step back, she gets to work, all business. She listens for sixty seconds, at least according to Billy who times her.

"It sounds normal to me, but I'll listen to mine to compare." She stands there, all serious, listening intently to her own heartbeat. She nods, removing the scope from her ears. "They sound the same. Now let's take your blood pressure."

She expertly straps the cuff to my arm and hits the button that tightens it.

"Ow!" I yelp. "It's like a boa constrictor is squeezing my arm."

"Hold still, Arie. It'll be over in a minute."

"Thanks for the sympathy. It's a good thing you're not planning to be a nurse," I grumble.

Angelina chooses to ignore me.

After the cuff loosens, she records the numbers in a little notebook. "120 over 79, perfect for girls our age."

"How do you know that?" Billy asks.

"I used Mom's computer to look it up."

Impatiently, I cross my arms and tap my foot, though it doesn't have the impact I intend, tapping on the soft sand. "Are you two finished?"

"We need to time you under water," Billy reminds me.

"But Nessie isn't here. I don't think I can do it without Nessie," I whine.

"Come on, Arie, just try," he wheedles, his brow crinkling, his mouth puckering into a pout. "You did it when that wave knocked you off the board."

"Okay," I relent, unable to deny him, "but only for a little while. Then we have to look for Harry and Trevor." Reluctantly pulling off my sweatshirt and shorts, I stalk to the gently rolling swells, wade in, and dive under the first wave.

Once I'm in and swimming, I forget about Billy, Angelina, and everything else, lost in the wonder of the undersea world. I glide along the ocean floor, eyes wide open. A small, two-spotted octopus fingers its way along the bottom, a swirl of cream and russet, its two brilliant blue spots acting as eyes to fool predators. A surprised crab scuttles sideways under a rock while a school of bright yellow garibaldi fish darts above me in perfect synch, scattering when I swim up toward them.

More than ever, I appreciate Mrs. Krenwinkel's enthusiastic sea-life lectures. She was right. It's another realm most people never bother to explore.

Spotting a marine snail called a Spanish Dancer, I dive down to get a closer look. I'd seen pictures of these colorful sea slugs in our science book but never a live one. It's as long as my hand, but some can grow to a foot. Its dark gold, thick, finger-like branches burst into a riot of neon blue. Light filtering through the water sets everything aglow. Graceful bat rays and playful dolphins, magenta rockfish and flat-faced halibut keep me amused until I finally feel the need to breathe and lazily make my way to the surface near the beach.

I have no idea how long I've been under—minutes, hours, or days; all time disappears when I'm in the ocean.

On the shore, Billy holds his stopwatch high as he jumps up and down. Angelina hops in excited circles.

"Wow!! You were under for twenty minutes!" Angelina shouts, furiously waving her stethoscope in the air.

"You're amazing, Arie!" Billy grabs both my hands and starts to pull me to him." As he realizes what he's doing, he lets go like I'm a hot potato, and glances at Angelina, who doesn't seem to notice. "You should train for the Olympics."

She straps the blood pressure cuff on my arm, pumps it, and then listens to my chest while Billy starts timing.

Angelina steps back, removes the scope from her ears, and stares at me like a puzzled puppy. "Everything's normal. Exactly the same as before you went in the water."

"So?" I don't understand why she's looking at me with that odd expression, like I'm a new animal she's discovered.

"After exercise, it should be higher. It's like you haven't exercised at all." With one elbow resting on her arm, a thumb cradling her chin, she taps an index finger along her cheek, studying me like an exotic specimen.

"I guess I'm in good shape, then, right? Can we stop all this now and go look for Trevor and Harry?"

They must notice my exasperation because they look at each other, nod, and start packing up their gear while I towel off and throw a sweatshirt on over my wet bathing suit. The sun will soon have us all searching for the shade.

"I have an idea that might help win Marni over," I say, "but it's not something I like."

Billy turns his face to me with that lopsided grin. "Do tell."

"Shopping." I drop it as if it's a bomb about to explode.

Billy laughs and Angelina snickers.

"But you hate shopping," Billy says.

"Yeah, but most girls love it, so I assume Marni might." I shrug.

"You're right. If you ask her to take you, it'll make her feel special, like you're her pal," Angelina says.

"But what if I don't like her?" I close one eye against the sun and sigh.

Angelina flashes her don't-be-a-dummy expression. "That doesn't matter. *Pretend.* Just be nice. She'll be so relieved, she'll *want* to believe you. It's easy. I've done it lots of times with guys my mom dates. They want to get in good with you, so they don't try too hard to find out if you like them."

"But I don't know if I can pull it off. You're a better actress than me, so you can get away with anything."

"You can do it, Arie. Just ask her advice on clothes and stuff."

"But I *hate* shopping." The memory of bra shopping still makes me cringe. "Izzie orders most of my stuff online. She'll know I'm faking."

"True. But she'll be proud of you for trying. And Marni won't know you hate shopping or that you're not like other girls," Billy adds.

I digest Billy's words. I guess some girls would be insulted, but it makes me proud.

"You're right about Izzie," I admit. Billy knows her almost as well as I do.

A day of shopping with a strange woman who's trying to take Dad away. Brilliant. But it might work. I guess it can't hurt.

***

In Shaw's Cove, we spot Trevor digging trenches in the sand. He glances up and breaks into a grin and darts toward us. He grabs my hand and tugs me forward. "Where have you guys been? Harry's looking for you!"

"Harry's looking for *us*?" I say as Trevor drags me across the sand, the others following. I spot Harry, melding into the rocks, slouching on a tattered blanket in the shade, his pet squirrel, Penia, on his shoulder. She's busy grubbing through Harry's mess of hair as if looking for a treat. She'll probably find one. There's no telling what's hidden in there.

Harry's chalk-white skin and slumped body send off alarm bells in my brain. When he raises his head, weary eyes, dull as dirt, gaze into mine.

"Are you all right, Harry? Do you need something to eat?" I rush on. "I can run back home and get you something. I'm so sorry. We got busy surfing, and . . ."

"Don't worry, little lady. Izzie's been taking care of me. You're just being a kid. I have something for you." He reaches into his shirt and brings out a scuffed, wrinkled envelope and hands it to me.

I take it, turning it over, looking for clues. "What is it?"

He snorts. "Open it and find out."

He sounds more like the old Harry, and I relax a little. A small, roundish bump interrupts the smoothness in the envelope's surface. When I open it and peer inside, a small abalone pearl huddles in the corner next to a delicate, creamy piece of paper. I pick out the pearl and hold it up so the others can see. Angelina and Billy hang back, silent. Pocketing it, I unfold the note. The now familiar handwriting causes me to sink to my knees. As I read the words, I can barely breathe.

Aurora. Meet me in Fisherman's Cove at midnight. Alone.

Trevor crowds in and starts asking questions. "What's that? Can I see?"

Angelina takes charge. Holding out her hand, she says, "Why don't you show me your trenches."

He takes her hand, easily distracted, excited to show off his creation.

Billy sits down next to me. "Are you okay?" He places one hand to my face, smoothing a strand of hair behind my ear.

Wordlessly, I hand him the note.

Holding the note in one hand, he says, "You can't go alone, Arie."

"But she said to come alone!"

"We don't know for sure who it is. Or even if it's a she. I'm going with you."

"Okay," I relent, "but you have to stay hidden. If it is Mom, I don't want to scare her off."

"Deal." He stands, brushing the sand off his hands. "But what about Angelina?"

"Not a problem. She's spending the night at her grandmother's house," I answer. I shove the note and pearl in my pocket. "I'll just tell her the note is the Harry nonesense."

I remember Harry and turn to him. "Harry, if you wrote this note, you need to tell me right now!"

"I've got better things to do than write a note to some sniveling kid." The blanket muffles his voice.

He doesn't look good, not at all. "Are you okay?"

His head pops up, like he's been napping. Penia stares at me with solemn eyes. *Something's not right* she seems to be telling me.

Can I also hear squirrels talk in my head? I try to shake off the feeling. It's too crazy to think about right now.

"I'm fine. Stop fussing." Harry waves us away, then drops his head onto his chest. Penia retreats into the frayed collar of Harry's shirt.

Chapter 20

Billy and I slip quietly down the path, the full moon lighting our way, glowing a silver trail across the dark ocean. I check my phone. Almost midnight.

"Stay here, Billy," I whisper. "I'm supposed to be alone."

"I'll watch to make sure you're safe," he whispers back as he crouches behind the Hawthorn bushes next to the stairs.

"And turn off the cell phone," I hiss, "or it might ruin everything."

He nods.

I turn mine off, slip out of my flip-flops, hook them between my fingers, and walk determinedly to the shoreline. The cold sand, the fishy smells, the cool mist on my tongue—I inhale it all. Maybe I should be afraid, but I'm not. It feels like I've waited for this moment my entire life. The gentle waves lap at my ankles. I could stand here forever.

And then the familiar, haunting lullaby shimmers the air. Shivering in anticipation, I strain to catch the words.

> I see the moon, the moon sees me,
> Shining through the branches of the old oak tree.
> Oh, let the light that shines on me,
> Shine on the one I love.

It's the voice I've never forgotten, the voice I still hear singing in my dreams. The words surface, the ones I'd tried to forget. My voice wavers and cracks as I sing back:

> Over the mountains, over the sea,
> Back where my heart is longing to be.
> Oh, let the light that shines on me,
> Shine on the one I love.

She climbs down from behind the rocky shelf that juts out over the ocean, a vision, her dark hair streaked with gold shining in the moonlight. It hangs almost to her knees, only a little shorter than the loose-fitting white dress she wore the last day I saw her. The memory of this little detail bubbles up from the recesses of my mind where I'd tucked it way, afraid of hope. Her dark eyes, moistened with unshed tears, are full of love.

Wrapping her arms around my shoulders, she pulls me close, kissing the top of my head. My arms encircle her waist, and the hot tears come. Leaning back, Mom cups my face in her hands. Kisses soft as butterfly wings mop away the saltiness staining my face.

"Do you remember the rest of the song, Aurora? Will you sing it with me, like we used to when you were little?" Her voice still has a that lilting, Irish sound.

I gulp back tears as her eyes look into my soul. Taking both my hands in hers, she begins to sing. I join in.

> I hear the lark, and the lark hears me
> Singing from the branches of the old oak tree.
> Oh, let the lark that sings to me
> Sing to the one I love.

"Where have you been, Mom?" I ask, my joy at having found her battling with anger.

"I've been right here, watching you grow up, keeping an eye on you." Her eyes implore me to understand.

"But *why*?" I cry out. "Why didn't you stay with *me* . . . and Dad?"

"That's a long story, one you deserve to hear. When I'm finished, I hope you'll understand why I had to leave," she speaks gently. Dropping one hand, she links our arms, turning us toward the sea. We stand for a while, lost in the magic of being.

Then all the tangled emotions unravel until there is only anger. I jerk my arm away.

"Nothing you can say changes the fact that you left," I accuse, practically shouting. "How could you do it?" The last part comes out as a sob.

"You are right. It was terrible what I did. I wouldn't blame you if you never forgive me. But please hear me out, that's all I ask. Then, if you never want to see me again, I'll understand."

I see the tears trickling down her face, but my heart is like stone. But I want to know what could've meant more to her than me. Sullenly, I agree to listen.

Let's find a comfortable place to sit. The breeze will pick up soon, bringing the chill with it." She turns around and yells, "You can come out now, Billy. Everything's all right."

My jaw drops, and Billy stands up, stepping out from behind his hiding spot. "How did you know he was there?" I ask.

"I've been watching you, remember. He seems like a nice boy. But send him home so we can talk."

Billy strides toward us, pulling himself up to his full size, frowning.

When he reaches us, Mom asks, "Can you keep our little secret, Billy?"

"Who are you?" he demands.

"I'm her mother," she states.

He examines our faces and grudgingly admits, "Yeah, you have the same eyes and hair." He crosses his arms over his chest, trying, I suppose, to appear manly.

"Aurora and I need time alone to get reacquainted. You can go home now. But I need your promise that you won't tell anyone."

He's in his ax murderer pose, so I place a hand gently on his arm, and he looks down at me.

"It's okay, Billy," I tell him. I turn to Mom, "He'll keep our secret."

"Are you sure, Arie?" he asks. "It doesn't seem right, leaving you here like this."

"I'm sure," I nod at him, trying to sound reassuring.

He turns to Mom. "She let you get away with calling her Aurora, so I guess it's all right." He sniffs, raising a defiant chin.

Mom laughs, her voice as musical as I remember. "I'll see her home safe."

"Okay. Text me when you get home, Arie?"

"Sure." He turns to go but looks back about halfway across the beach. I give him a little wave of reassurance; he half-heartedly waves back.

Mom leads me to a crevice against the cliff face, the same one Harry uses when the tide's out. We settle in, backs leaning against the hard rock.

"I know you must have a lot of questions, so I'll start at the beginning. Did your dad ever tell you how we met?" Her voice carries a sliver of irritation.

"No. He won't talk about it, but Izzie said you met in Ireland, while he was on a business trip. You fell in love, got married, and came back here."

"I'm so grateful for Isabel," she says, looking wistfully out on the ocean. "That story is partially true," she nods, "but not the whole story."

Mystified, I wait for enlightenment.

She takes a deep breath and begins her story. "We did meet and fall in love in Ireland. But I didn't come back with him voluntarily—at least not entirely."

Shocked into silence, I wait.

"What I'm about to tell you will sound fantastic, unreal, but I promise by the time you leave here, you'll believe it. Aurora, have you ever heard Irish legends of the selkies?"

Startled at the abruptness of this last remark, I turn my head and stare at her. "Yes," I manage to stammer. "I saw a movie about them."

"In the stories, a selkie, or seal, is somewhat like a mermaid. Selkies can remove their skins and be human."

"So? What's *that* got to do with you running away from me?"

She ignores my bitter tone and continues. "Like mermaids, humans find selkies irresistible. One story says that if a human can steal a selkie's skin, it must do as the human bids it."

"I still don't get it. What are you talking about?" I stand up and look down at her.

"Aurora, please sit down. You said you'd listen." Her voice and eyes are calm, but she wraps a lock of hair around her fingers.

"That's another thing, why did you give me that stupid name? It's all you left me, and I hate it." I fling the words at her.

"I named you for the aurora borealis, the northern lights, one of the most beautiful sights on earth." She just sits there, gazing up at me.

"Oh." I wish I could think of some stinging remark, but instead, I sit back down.

"There is no easy way to put this," she says, twisting her hair more furiously now, "so I'll just say it. I'm a selkie."

I jump up, "You don't mean . . . but that's crazy!" I

look around, wild-eyed, wishing I hadn't sent Billy away. Maybe she has schizophrenia like Harry and Uncle Al. She might be dangerous.

"Please," she pleads. "I told you it sounds unbelievable, but if you look in your heart, you'll know it's the truth."

Slowly, I sink to the ground. Everything has taken on a dream quality—the moon-drenched night, her lyrical voice, the sound of waves lapping at the sand. I tuck my knees up to my chest for protection and think about the last few months. It all begins to make an unbelievable type of sense—the pearls, the sand writing, Trevor's sightings, Harry's mysterious mutterings. And my superpower in the water, and the way I can hear what animals think. But it's impossible!

After what seems an eternity, I respond, "Okay, tell me the rest." I find myself leaning slightly away from her, worried that she's a mental case—and afraid she might be telling the truth.

"Your dad was still working on his double doctorate in mythology and anthropology when I met him. He came to Ireland to finish the last part of his thesis, connecting the legends of water creatures from around the world: merfolk, Sumerian water deities, water nymphs—and of course, selkies. He never expected to find a real one." She smiles at her memory.

I shiver, and she pulls me close, her body surprisingly warm and smelling of the sea. My mind tells me to pull away but my heart wins and I snuggle into her, a perfect fit.

"Walking on the beach one morning in my human form, I saw him gazing out to sea. He was so handsome." She says it so matter-of-factly that it doesn't sound at all unnatural for her to be talking about her *human form*. "He came out of his trance as I walked past. He smiled that lazy, crooked smile of his, and I fell for him in an instant."

"I know that look, but he hasn't smiled much since you left," I accuse as I break the embrace and scoot a few inches away. Except since he met Marni. I shove that problem aside for now.

Conflicting emotions—love and hate, joy and sorrow, anger and dismay—confuse my body, which can't decide whether to hold onto her forever or run as far away as possible.

Her crestfallen face tells me the dart hit its mark, but I just glare at her, thinking about the dark circles under Dad's eyes, his feeble attempts to appear happy for all those years, his greying hair.

"I'm so sorry, Aurora," she says, "I never meant to hurt either of you. I couldn't help it. He stole my soul; I needed it back."

Her soul? What does that mean? I keep my knees tucked to my chest and rest my sullen chin on them, waiting for her to resume her tale.

Taking a deep breath, she begins again on the exhale, "Every day, I'd shed my seal-self, hiding the skin in a little cave in the rocks. When I'd climb over, he'd be waiting. We spent wonderful days, strolling on the beach hand-in-hand, getting to know one another. We'd talk about the ancient stories and argue about their meanings. Then he'd take me to a cozy little pub for supper where we'd eat boiled shrimp and drink Irish beer.

After a month, he asked me to marry him. As much as it hurt, as fiercely as I loved him, I had to tell him no. It was impossible! How could I explain it to him? For selkies, the ocean is part of them, their soul. It's a *necessity*, like breathing."

My sharp intake of air and sudden stiffness alert her.

"Yes," she gently answers my unspoken question, "I'm the seal you call Nessie."

The tears come again, along with choked sobs. I wipe my leaking face on the sleeve of my sweatshirt. She *has* been here all the time, looking out for me. Either that, or we're both crazy. Or maybe I'm trapped in a long dream.

Mom reaches out, caressing my shoulder. "I've never left you, Aurora, not really."

"Then why did you wait until now to tell me?" I ask, tucking my sweatshirt over my knees for comfort, drawing into a shell like a hermit crab.

"I'm getting to that, sweetie."

I nod, and she resumes.

"After I told your father I couldn't marry him, I fled over the rocks, grabbed my skin, and disappeared into the water. I heard him calling my name, trying to follow. It broke my heart to leave him. I watched from the water every day for a week as he scanned the rocks, pacing back and forth, hoping I'd change my mind and return. Finally, he quit showing up. I thought it safe to go ashore again. I wanted to walk alone and remember him, to grieve what could never be.

When I climbed back over the rocks, there he was, waiting, holding my seal skin. He knew the legend, you see, had been suspicious, so he'd followed me one night and watched me put on my skin. He knew that I'd have to go with him. I begged him not to make me leave my home, the sea, told him that I'd surely not survive if I had to live on land. He refused to believe it, told me we'd be happy together, he'd buy a little cottage by the ocean. I loved him so much that I finally agreed to go with him."

"But that's so cruel!" I say, choking on my fury at Dad, at the anger and incredible pain he'd caused, and furious at her for leaving us.

"He didn't realize how cruel he was being," she says, her tone wistful and forgiving. "And I loved him so much I wanted to believe it could work. He dismissed my fears, my pleas, and so I went with him. He brought me to Laguna Beach and hid my skin, afraid I would return to the sea."

"What? He *hid* it from you. But that's horrible!" I had trouble picturing my gentle dad being so mean.

"You'll understand more about love when you're older, what it can make a person do. I've forgiven him. Selkies inspire a love so strong, it's like an enchantment. Anyway, I was happy for a while, but I searched for my skin whenever he went to work. I almost went mad trying to find it; I ached to return to the ocean, even an unfamiliar one. But I also longed to stay." She shakes her head as if trying to clear the memories. "What an impossible situation."

Her eyes fill with tears and I want so much to make her feel better. I scooch closer, inhaling her lovely, sea-drenched scent.

"After you were born, I thought I could do it. You were my little miracle, the glue that held my sanity. I tried to give up the daily searches and focus on motherhood. I almost succeeded. But I grew so depressed, so despondent. Nothing helped, not even medication. I needed the one thing your father wouldn't give me—myself. She sits there, gazing out on the moonlit water. "What happened next, Mom?" I ask, afraid of the shard of a memory working its way out of my mind.

"You found it for me." She whispers the words, barely audible.

The memory clicks into place, clear as the moonlit night. "Behind the shed, hidden in a box under the rocks." Burying my head in my knees, I say through my muffled sobs, "It's all my fault! If I hadn't found it, you wouldn't have left." Mom takes me in her arms. I remember the day vividly now, the bright afternoon sun, how I took refuge in the shade of the shed, digging for buried treasure—and then I'd found it. Mom had come out to check on me. I hadn't been able to pull the box all the way out of the ground. She'd dropped to her knees and torn at the dirt, digging with her hands, then wrenched off the lid, lifted it out of its hiding hole, and cradled it next to her face, inhaling. Kneeling down, she hugged me, murmuring "Thank you, baby," kissing my face.

Then she dropped me off at Izzie's.

"It's not your fault, honey, don't ever think that. You gave me back my life. I was already dead inside. Eventually, I would have died physically as well. I had been getting weaker every day. That's what your father refused to understand. I don't blame him, either. He loved me. I loved him. He just couldn't accept that some things can never be. To lose one's soul is to lose one's life. I had to go back to the sea. I'm a wild creature and belong in the wild."

We sit for a while, her arm around me, my head still buried in my sleeves. She raises my face with her hands, turns it to her, and kisses the tip of my nose. "I'll always love you, Aurora. And your father. But he and I can't be together."

Her face is so close I can almost hear the sorrow seeping from her mind. "What about me?" I ask in a small voice.

"That's one of the reasons I'm here—to explain what happens to selkie children born half human on land."

I just stare at the light on the ocean, afraid of the terrible reluctance in her voice.

"On their thirteenth birthdays, they must decide: stay on land and be human or join their seal families and live a life in the ocean."

Like ice water, it hits me full force. I'm part selkie. This can't be happening.

"But I'm almost thirteen!" I cry out.

"You still have some time. I'll help you understand the world in the ocean, what choice you'd be making, just as I've been doing as Nessie. Whatever you choose, I'll support your decision. I'm guessing you've already begun to feel the changes when you're in the ocean. Not needing to breathe for long periods of time. Growing faster, stronger, sleeker."

"Yes, but I thought …." I let the words trail off. Her eyes ooze sympathy.

"You thought it was just part of growing up?" she finishes for me. "I'm heart-broken, having to ask you to choose, but I it's my duty as a selkie and a mother. You deserve to know everything."

I bury my head again, stunned by the agonizing choice she's asking me to make. How can I leave Dad, Izzie, Billy, and Angelina? She broke Dad's heart; I can't do the same. Now I understand why he hates me going near the water, why he wants to move to Indiana, far from the ocean. But as much as I don't want to leave them, I want Mom back.

And Dad now has Marni.

"I'm sorry. Aurora. The last thing I ever wanted to do was hurt you. But by the laws of the sea, I have to offer you the chance to become your other self."

"What happens to me if I stay with Dad?"

"You'll be a land creature, better in the water than other humans, but you'll never completely become your seal-self." The words hover in the moist night.

"Can't you come back to us, Mom, *please!*"

She reaches over and strokes my hair. "That's not possible, love. I'm sorry."

Could it get any worse? We sit for a while, staring out at the water. "Who is the seal who helped me when I fell off my board?"

"My . . . mate."

I blow out the breath I'd been holding. They'll never be together. Mom has a husband and Dad has Marni. Sadness steals my voice. There's nothing more for me to say.

Mom stands up, holding out her hand. I take it, and she tugs me up. "I'd better get you home. We can start exploring day after tomorrow if you like. You need your rest tonight, being out so late. Can you be here that morning? The sooner you learn about our world, the better. I don't want you to make this decision without knowing what you'd be gaining—and what you'd be giving up."

I hang back, overwhelmed. Then nod. We begin walking up the hill, and I see Billy skulking under the banana trees.

Mom smiles. "It's okay, Billy, come walk with us. You're a good friend to watch out for Aurora. Thank you."

"Yes, ma'am." He stares at her in wonder.

Mom walks with us to the corner of my street and stops. "I'll wait here until you're in the house and then see Billy home."

"I just live around the block, Mrs. . . . . I mean . . .." he awkwardly trails off.

"You can call me Kalysta," she says, rescuing Billy.

"Kalysta," he repeats, her name sounding like an enchantment. "I'll jog home."

She turns to me, hugging me close, showering my face with kisses. Usually a display of affection in front of Billy would mortify me, but I'm not embarrassed.

"I'll see you soon," she murmurs against my hair then lets go.

Billy escorts me to the door, but I keep looking back, watching her under the light of the streetlamp, afraid she'll disappear, that it's somehow all been a dream.

Chapter 21

When I wake, it's late, past 8:00. I didn't think I could sleep, but Mom was right. I needed it. *Mom.* It's strange and wonderful, troubling and heart-wrenching, thinking about her, but oddly soothing. I have to believe everything will be all right or I'll go crazy.

I forgot to tell her about Dad trying to move me to Indiana. I'll tell her first thing tomorrow. Maybe she can help.

My phone buzzes. Billy has left seven messages, all saying essentially the same thing: "What did she say?"

I text back: *I don't want to write anything about her in a text. Let's go to the beach. I'll tell you then.*

He replies with what I imagine is a sullen *"Okay."*

Then, *"Angelina's coming, too."*

Downstairs, the stale coffee smell insults my senses. Dad has already left. Marni comes today.

Izzie's in the backyard, fussing in the garden. A wicker basket brimming with ripe tomatoes, lemons, chili peppers, green beans, and a variety of herbs squats in the grass beside her.

"Are you planning the Last Supper?" I joke.

She barks a short laugh and straightens up. "No. Just taking some of this to the teen shelter. Those poor children. I'm hoping this little harvest will encourage some of them to plant a garden. I'm teaching them how to grow things. It's food for the soul as well as the body."

Good ole' Izzie with the big heart.

"I love you, Izzie."

"I love you, too, Sugar Plum. Now come help me put this in the car." She gestures to another loaded basket on the ground. "Then I'll get you some breakfast. You're quite the slug-a-bed this morning. Did you stay up late texting Billy?" Her knowing smile makes me blush.

"Billy and I always stay up texting," I confess. I wish I could tell her what's *really* happening. But I know I can't. Besides, I doubt she'd believe me. I haven't even told Billy the *real* truth. How do you tell someone your mother is a seal?

After we load the baskets into the car, we return to the kitchen. Izzie takes a plate of whole grain pancakes out of the oven. "I kept these warm for you."

"You're the best, Izzie!" She ruffles my hair then turns to the sink while I heap my plate with a load of apricots, butter, and syrup and enthusiastically plow into the gooey mess. The rattle of dishes and running water makes a noisy musical accompaniment to my meal. Izzie's pancakes—Nirvana on a plate.

"Have you seen Harry lately, Sugar Plum?"

"We saw him yesterday at the beach. He didn't look so good. I'm a little worried," I answer, gulping down orange juice.

"Don't talk with your mouth full, Arie."

"Then don't ask me stuff while I'm eating." She's so distracted, she doesn't even notice my smart aleck remark.

"If you see him today, text and let me know where he is." Her worrying tone stops the forkful of goodness halfway to its destination.

"Okay." I put down my fork, still loaded, no longer hungry. A rock has lodged itself in my stomach. "Do you think something's wrong with him?"

"It's probably nothing, but I haven't been able to find him in his usual spots. I've packed an extra sandwich in case you see him," she says. "Try and get him to eat something. He's taken with you."

"Taken with me? What does that mean?"

"It means he likes you, and all you kids. Every time I see him, he's full of stories about the three of you. You talk to him like he's a human being. Most people don't bother. I'm proud of you, taking the time for an old homeless man, making him feel like he still matters."

"He does matter. We like him, too," I respond, though blushing a little at the praise. Izzie isn't exactly generous with the compliments, so it means a lot. It's one of the things I love about her. And I do mean it about Harry. He's helped me more than I can ever confess to Izzie.

"I'm glad." She dries her hands and unties her apron, hanging it on the hook by the back door, all business now. "Clean up your dishes. I'm heading over to the shelter."

I carry my plate to the sink while Izzie collects her purse and keys and heads to the door. She pauses and turns. "Oh, and Arie. Don't forget, your dad's friend arrives today." She's wearing her sternest expression. "You be nice, now. I'm counting on you."

"I'll be nice, all right." I use my wickedest smile.

She takes two steps toward me. "Now, see here, young lady, don't you do anything to scare the woman off."

"If she's going to be in Dad's life, I need to make her like me, that's all." It's fun to get a rise out of Izzie. The opportunity almost never happens. "Don't worry. I'll behave."

"You'd better!" She huffs out of the house.

Billy's locking his door when I arrive, and our boards are already leaning against the gate, ready to go. He glances around, and finding the coast clear, gives me a quick, soft kiss, tasting of Burt's Bees lip balm. He takes my hand as we head to the trolley to meet Angelina, surfboards tucked under our free arms.

Squeezing my hand, he says, "Tell me what she said last night. Is she going to help us so you won't have to move to Indiana?"

"I forgot to tell her about Indiana. But she did say I could maybe live with her if I want." I bite my lip at the fib.

"Where does she live?"

That's such a normal question, I hadn't even thought about how to answer it. I can't exactly tell him she lives in the sea.

"Um . . . I don't know for sure. Around here somewhere. She didn't say."

"You better find out!" Billy stops and faces me, forcing me to meet his eyes. "It won't do us any good if she lives in Siberia."

"I'm meeting her tomorrow. I'll find out then."

"Cool!" His hopeful expression makes my eyes sting.

"Should we tell Angelina?" he asks.

"Not just yet. But soon. There's a lot to figure out first, and Mom asked us to keep it secret, remember?"

"Yeah, you're right."

"You can't come tomorrow. I have to see Mom alone." I don't want to exclude Billy, but I have to.

"Why?" he asks, the question buzzing with curiosity.

"Because she's going to show me where she lives and doesn't want anyone else to know yet." I'm getting pretty good at this partial-truth thing. "It's just one day."

"Okay," he says, not sounding very happy, "If you say so." He lets go of my hand as we approach the trolley stop.

Angelina's sitting on the edge of the low cement wall by the trolley stop in front of Diver's Cove. She stands up as we get closer.

"You don't have to stop holding hands for my sake," she teases, her mouth turned up, eyes bright like she wants to laugh but is trying not to. "I already saw you. Besides, I figured it out a long time ago. You've been acting all goofy lately."

Billy and I exchange embarrassed glances.

"Okay, Sherlock Holmes," Billy says, defiantly grabbing my hand. "We're busted."

Angelina giggles with delight.

I'm just relieved it's out in the open. Keeping secrets makes me uneasy.

The trolley arrives, and we lug our boards to the back, chattering all the way to Thalia Street.

The perfect waves keep us in the water most of the morning. Exhausted, we paddle back to shore and flop in the sand, letting the warm sun bake us dry as we munch on pita sandwiches stuffed with fresh goodies from Izzie's garden, all slathered with homemade humus and shrimp tucked in among the green and yellow peppers, sweet tomatoes and herbs.

Lazily, we crowd into the trolley and make our way back to town and Fisherman's Cove to look for Harry. Propping our boards against the rocks where kayakers haphazardly store their rides, we roam the usual haunts, but can't find him anywhere. I text Izzie.

She texts back an abrupt okay, setting off alarm bells in my brain—no Sugar Plum, no admonishments to be home on time. She must really be worried about Harry.

We drift all afternoon, sometimes stopping to play Frisbee or scour the tide pools for ocean creatures.

At 4:00, the salt from the sea drying in flakes on our parched bodies, we grab our boards and ramble home. Angelina leaves us at the corner, and Billy and I walk slowly, stowing the boards at his house. Hand in hand, reluctant to part, he walks me to my house. When we reach my cottage, I drop his hand. Dad's home.

"Do you want me to go in with you?" Billy asks.

"Thanks, but I better go in alone." Time to face reality.

Billy looks relieved. I don't blame him. It's going to be awkward. We say goodbye, and I shuffle up the steps, trying to mold my face into something resembling a smile.

Soft laughter greets me as I quietly open the front screen and follow the sound to the back door. Dad and Marni sit at the patio table, sharing a bottle of red wine. I stand inside the screen, watching them for a while. They're so absorbed in each other, they don't realize I'm standing silently only ten feet away. One of Dad's hands covers hers as he smiles at something she says. She uses her other perfectly manicured hand to tuck a strand of light brown, shoulder length hair behind her ear. The dark pink polish matches her tank top and sandals, the toes identical to her nails, too matching, boring, and girlie. White cropped pants reveal slender calves. She's pretty enough, I suppose, in that Midwestern bland way like the tourists who flock to Laguna in the summer, but she doesn't come close to Mom's exotic beauty and athletic build. I resist the urge to wrinkle my nose in distaste.

As I open the door, they turn their heads in surprise, and Dad removes his hand from hers.

His wide smile and outstretched arms beckon me. "Arie, sweetheart! I'm so glad you're home. We've been waiting for you. Come meet Marni."

He's so happy I can barely stand it. But I smile anyway and go to him. He hugs me with one arm around my waist and I affectionately hug him back, planting a noisy kiss on his cheek, playing it up for Marni.

My insides churn, angry at him for what he did to Mom. I can't very well say anything about it with an intruder visiting.

"It's so good to meet you!" Marni gushes, reaching out a hand.

Her weak, girlie grip tells me more than I want to know. This may need better acting skills than I'm capable of. There won't be any Academy Awards in my future. Biting the inside of my cheek, I firmly shake her hand while looking her straight in the eye with more confidence than I feel.

"Sit down and tell me all about yourself!"

Oh brother. I hate when people try too hard in that phony-baloney way. I perch on the edge of the seat Dad pulls between them for me.

"So, you're on summer break. What do you do with yourself all day?"

Her chirpy voice makes me cringe, but I paste on a smile and respond with an equally fake chirp, "Mostly hanging out with my friends at the beach. I *love* the beach. I can't imagine ever living away from the ocean."

Okay, so not my finest moment, but I couldn't resist.

Dad slides a sideways, warning eye at me. I put on my angel face and smile as sweetly as I can.

"That sounds so nice," she says, the chirp weaker now, deflated by my not-so-subtle dig. "Maybe you can show me your favorite spots while I'm here."

"Okay! You'll love it here." I warm to this idea and chatter on for a few minutes about the different coves, the surfers and divers, Harry. This part, I don't have to fake.

"Great! When should we go?" she asks but doesn't sound like her heart is in it.

"How about day after tomorrow? After, we can get ice cream and maybe go shopping!" The shopping I have to fake, but her eyes light up, so I know I've hooked her.

"Dad, can we take her to watch the sunset? *Please*," I beg.

"I don't see why not," he answers, his eyes all soft and mushy. "What do you think, Marni? Are you up to seeing a fabulous sunset?"

I cringe at his easy acceptance. I thought for sure he'd say no. He'll go to the beach for Marni but not for *me*.

She claps her hands. "That sounds lovely!"

"We have a couple of hours, Dad. Did you get P.F. Chang's? I can heat it up and we can eat out here." I hope I don't sound too enthusiastic. Luckily, Dad's so happy, I doubt he notices my overly eager behavior. Though I catch Marni casting a doubting glance my way.

"Let me help you, sweetie," Dad says, starting to get up.

"No, you stay here with Marni and finish your drinks. I'll get it."

He settles back in his seat while I high-tail it out of there, relieved to have something to do so I don't have to keep up the charade of being nice to Marni. Ick.

I retrieve the containers from the fridge—Kung Pao shrimp, garlic long beans, and fluffy white rice. While it heats in the microwave, I get out the good dishes, napkins, and flatware and set the patio table, maneuvering around them while they sip wine and chat.

While we eat, they mostly talk about work while I bolt my food as fast as I can.

"Can I go take a shower now, Dad? I'm itchy from the sand."

"Sure, kiddo, but hurry. We don't want to miss the sunset."

I start to gather plates, but Marni says, "I'll get that, sweetie, you go get ready."

Sweetie? Who is she to call me sweetie? I just met her. Izzie's stern face rises in my mind like a ghost, so I smile and say, "Thank you, Marni. That's nice of you."

All this forced smiling makes my jaw ache.

The shower provides sanctuary from my troubles. The warm water and lavender soap rinse away the smells of the sea, calming my jangled nerves. I think best in the shower and come up with the idea to ask Billy and Angelina to "accidentally" run into us at the beach. They both swiftly reply to my text, enthusiastic about making Marni an ally in our plan to keep me from being exiled to outer Mongolia.

Emerging from my room, refreshed and relieved that the troops are coming to my rescue, I tug on a sweatshirt over my "Soft Kitty" t-shirt from *The Big Bang Theory*. Marni and Dad have the kitchen cleaned so well it would pass even Izzie's inspection.

"What an adorable sweatshirt!" Marni exclaims. "Where did you get it?"

She's pouring it on a little thick. It's just a dumb old sweatshirt, green and worn, with the store's faded pink logo on the front, but I try to match her enthusiasm. "I'm glad you like it! I got it at Thalia Surf Shop. I'll take you there

. . . if you want." I try to say this last part with a tinge of hope, like I really want her to go with me.

I really hate myself right now.

"I'd love that!" she says. "I'm sure you know all the best stores in town."

"She knows this town better than I do," Dad brags. "She'll be a great tour guide."

Giving Dad an encouraging push toward the door, I complain, "Let's *go* or we'll miss the sunset."

"Okay, okay, hold your horses," he laughs.

I've never heard him laugh so much. Resentment tries to thieve its way into my heart.

We hustle down the hill, me in the lead, Dad and Marni holding hands and trying to keep up. We cross the street and stop for a few minutes at the gazebo. Marni chatters on about its "charm."

From this vantage point, I can watch for the troops. Spotting them on the sidewalk, heading toward Main Beach (where I told them to meet us), I say, "Look, Dad! It's Billy and Angelina. Can we catch up with them?"

"You run along. We'll follow and meet you at Main Beach," Dad agrees, exchanging smiles with Marni.

Blech.

"Thanks, Dad!" I take off at a run. "Billy, Angelina, wait up!"

They stop and wait as I huff up.

"How's it going with *Marni?*" Angelina asks.

"Yeah, do you like her?" Billy chimes in.

"She's okay, I guess. The shopping idea worked. I'm taking her on a tour of the town day after tomorrow."

"Great! Everything's going as planned." Billy nods.

Main Beach swarms with people, all getting ready for the big 4th of July celebration tomorrow. It's a perfect summer evening, balmy but with a cool summer breeze. No clouds mar the sky. The sun slowly makes its way toward the horizon, a bright orange ball turning the water turquoise.

We're standing along the shore, the water swirling around our feet, when Dad and Marni join us.

"Hi, Mr. McGinnis." Billy's voice has the right amount of casualness, putting everyone at ease.

Dad introduces Marni, and we all sit in the sand facing the sun, waiting for the show.

Billy peppers Marni with questions about Indiana, how she likes Laguna Beach, keeping her occupied so I don't have to.

Angelina keeps up her end of the bargain, saying to Marni, "You're going to love it here so much you'll never want to leave."

Marni warms to her—no one can resist Angelina the Angel. Not many know her more devilish accomplishments like forgery and stealing her mom's work password.

"I'm sure I will, Angelina. Arie's going to show me around day after tomorrow. Maybe you can join us? We can make it a girl's day out."

Angelina turns to me, the question in her eyes.

"That's a great idea, Marni," I say, grateful for Angelina's help and Marni's suggestion. She must be as unnerved as I am about spending a day just the two of us. "Can you, Angelina? Please?"

"Thank you, ma'am," she says, all sweetness. "I'll ask my mom, but I'm sure she won't mind."

The little faker. I almost laugh.

"That's settled, then. We'll let you know what time," Marni says, taking charge.

Dad grins from ear-to-ear and puts his arm casually around Marni's shoulders. She smiles up at him. Though it hurts, they seem so happy my jealousy and meanness dissolve a little.

We sit in silence, enjoying the last sliver of the sun sink behind Catalina Island, leaving a golden halo on the hills.

Chapter 22

The minute we get home, I flee to my room to sit and fiddle with my pearl necklace, thinking of Mom, and then I text back and forth with Angelina and Billy. At 10:00, I climb into bed, switch off the light, and read for an hour until I hear the door shut and footsteps on the gravel driveway. I shouldn't spy out the window but do it anyway and watch as Dad kisses Marni by the gate at the end of the driveway under the streetlight. Then he opens the car door, his hand on the small of her back as he helps her in. They drive away, leaving me alone.

Tossing and turning, my heart heavy and my soul agitated, I finally drop off to a light sleep until Dad comes home at 3:30. He tries to be quiet but doesn't succeed, his footsteps squeaking every board of the hardwood floor. I listen until the house falls silent again then struggle to go back to sleep but can't get the picture of them kissing out of my head.

At 5:00, I give up and dress in the dark. Using my cell phone as a flashlight, I creep into the kitchen, stuff a few snacks in my backpack, and leave a note saying I'm at the cove with Billy and Angelina. Billy promised to cover for me while I spend the day with Mom. They're going to surf and meet me in the afternoon at Fisherman's Cove.

Though it's a little spooky sneaking through the quiet Laguna Beach streets all alone in the dark, I'm not afraid. I know Mom's waiting for me. My mind can't make sense of my body's emotions. Anxiety rules my muscles but my mind vibrates with excitement.

Mom. Such a simple word.

A bold coyote crossing PCH startles me. I freeze. Its aggressive stance causes my heart to thump like a drum, but then her lyrical Irish voice is there. "Aurora, stay very still, honey."

I let out a breath of relief as I spot her. Soft words unlike any I've heard float in the air. The coyote's ears perk up. It seems to understand as it tucks its tail between its legs and slinks off, disappearing into the shadowed streets.

Then she's there, her arms around me, protecting. I fold into her, letting her warmth comfort me.

"Don't be afraid, Aurora. I won't let anything harm you."

Burrowing into her distinctive ocean scent, I don't ever want to let go. I've never felt so safe.

Am I betraying Dad, feeling this way, wanting to be with her? "I've missed you so much, Mom." The muffled words struggle up from my face nestled against her neck.

She gently puts her hands on my shoulders and pushes back, smiling. "Are you ready?"

I nod. She takes my hand, and we walk slowly to Fisherman's Cove.

"What were those words you said to the coyote?" I ask. "You did talk to it, didn't you?"

"It's not talk, exactly," she replies. "It's more of a series of sounds that most mammals understand." She frowns, as if searching for the right words to explain. "Let's just say I gave him the impression that he'd be sorry if he made another move toward you."

"I wish I knew how to do that. Can you teach me?"

"It should come to you naturally," she answers. "Have you noticed any unusual experiences around animals? As if you understand their thoughts?"

"Yes!" Now it makes sense when I thought I could read Harry's squirrel's warning about Harry. I tell her what happened.

She nods. "If you listen carefully, you'll be able to understand some of what an animal tells you, even if you don't become a full selkie."

Then Mom changes the subject before I can ask her more about it.

"It must be the Fourth of July." She gestures at the decorations on the lampposts. Her face has a faraway, yearning look. "I had forgotten about that uniquely American holiday. We'll have to be on the lookout. People will swarm the beaches early today, saving their spots for the big show. Do you have plans?"

"Yeah." I pause. "We're going to barbecue and then watch fireworks."

"That's nice." By now we're on the sand. She stops.

"Mom?"

"Yes, sweetheart, what is it?"

"I have something to tell you."

"You can tell me anything, Aurora." She waits, letting me find the words.

I blurt out, "Dad has a girlfriend and wants to make me move to Indiana." She's so quiet, I think I've said something wrong.

"Mom?" The question lingers in the balmy still-dark morning. I try to decipher the look on her face. Her mouth drawn tight, her eyes flashing fire in the moonlight. It's definitely anger. It seethes below the surface, ready to erupt. It's an almost frightening look.

"Yes. Harry told me," she says. "He has no right. I knew he was capable of this type of behavior, but I never thought he'd go this far. You are my daughter, whether he likes it or not, and he is bound by the rules."

"What rules?"

"Selkie rules." She explains that by marrying a selkie, a human must agree to let the children make the choice when they turn thirteen. Dad had agreed.

"What are we going to do?"

"I don't know but try not to worry. We'll think of something. For now, let me show you your new world. If you'll give me your clothes, I'll put them where they'll keep dry and no one will find them."

I peel them off, my swimsuit underneath, and hand them to her. Neatly, Mom rolls them into a tight bundle and slides them into a light green bag that smells of the sea. Then I realize what it is—a giant kelp bladder. I've never seen one so big.

"Wait here," she tells me, "I'll be right back." She dives into a gentle wave, still wearing the white dress that clings like a third skin, and disappears for a few minutes, then pops up out of the water just beyond the break line, still as Mom. As soon as I see her wave, I dash in, trying to imitate her graceful entry. I'm a little clumsy, but she cheers me anyway.

"You're getting quite good, Aurora! Come on, let's explore."

"How come you're not Nessie?" I thought for sure she'd reappear as my beautiful seal.

"It's better this way in case someone spots us. They'll just see a mother and daughter, having a swim."

"Oh. I hadn't thought of that."

At her signal, we flip over and submerge, seal-like, down to the bottom of the sea. We glide along for about an hour but keep close to shore, heading south, rising occasionally to breathe, floating on our backs in bliss on the surface, watching the sun as it slowly emerges behind the hills.

"Where are we?" I ask.

"Near Dana Point. Your father and I used to bring you here when you were little to watch the boats sailing in and out of the harbor."

She gazes at the sunrise, and we continue to rest on the water, contented.

"Now that the sun's up, you'll be able to see better." Mom turns to me, her face radiant.

She looks so at peace, exactly where she belongs.

"Maybe we better start back," she suggests. "Too many people about. I'll show you a few special spots along the way. We can visit deeper water another time."

Slowly, she dives under and I follow, enjoying the tingling of the saltwater on my skin, the bright colors now visible in the sun's rays.

Suddenly, Mom takes my hand and darts down toward a patch of orange glowing on the ocean floor. As we close in, I see what they are—anemones, the color of Cream-sickles, clustered on a dark rock, dozens of them, their white feelers floating lazily in the light current. A little farther, another patch of anemones—white, with mushroom-like stalks, their caps like downy feathers—cling to the sides of the rocks, waving in the water like friendly bystanders. As we skim the edge, we see red sponges and purple jellyfish, soft pink cup corals and red sea urchins, all bright under the summer sun softly filtering through the saltwater.

Sensing something behind us, I turn, just as a dolphin, as startled as I am, almost plows into me. Laughing with relief, I reach out, and it lets me touch its sleek, long beak, marking it as a Common Dolphin. Several more surround us, a small pod of five, and we swim with them, delighted by their company as they take turns rushing to the surface, flipping and twisting, diving and dancing. Suddenly, they're off like torpedoes.

Cheered by their silly antics, I glide beside Mom, happy as we explore along the way home.

When we finally reach Fisherman's Cove, the sun is high in the sky.

"Paddle to shore, sweetie, like you're just having a swim. I'll get your clothes and meet you on the rocks."

I swim in. Locals already dot the tiny cove, making the most of the spectacular day, their umbrellas and chairs, coolers and towels, decorating the sand in an array of bright colors. No one seems to notice as I drag my tired limbs out of the water and clamber up onto the rocks. When I get to the middle, I see her, walking along the water's edge in Shaw's Cove, her sleek, wet hair curling around her. She's carrying my small bundle of clothes, holding it close to her chest.

Somehow, she looks different than when in the water, not quite comfortable.

She doesn't belong here. The realization shakes me to the roots. She'll never live on land. But can I live in the sea?

Mom climbs up beside me, and we sit for a while, our faces turned to the water. My brain trolls for answers but has no luck.

I can't leave Dad, Billy, Izzie, and Angelina—everything and everyone I know and love. Except Mom. I can't lose her, either. But Dad means Indiana. Either choice means a terrible loss.

Anguish weights me down, and I find it hard to breathe. Afraid of the answer, I can't bear to ask the question. What will happen if I can't talk Dad out of Indiana? Will I never see her again?

And then it comes to me, the answer to my dilemma. If I threaten Dad that I'm going to go with Mom, then he'll have to stay here or never see me again. My mood brightens as my mind plots and schemes.

Mom looks at me with the wisdom of the ages, as if understanding my innermost thoughts. "I'd better go, honey, so your friends don't worry. I know you have a big day ahead."

Instead of telling her my plan, I ask, "Can we do it again, Mom? Explore, I mean?"

Her troubled face lightens just a little, her eyes more relaxed. "Of course. When can you get away?"

"Day after tomorrow, I think. I don't know what Dad has planned with Marni here." I itch with impatience, having to delay seeing Mom because of Marni.

"I'll be here at the usual time. If you can't make it, I'll understand. She reaches over, gives me a big hug, then rises, and dives into the ocean. I wait to see if she'll surface, but she's gone.

If I can't get Marni to move here, I'll blackmail Dad, but only as a last resort.

I throw my sweatshirt on over my damp suit and climb down to the sand. Billy and Angelina have set up an umbrella, sand chairs, and beach towels, staking our claim.

Angelina gives me a quizzical look. "What were you doing on the rocks?"

"Uh . . . I had a swim with Nessie and came ashore in Shaw's Cove. I thought I might see Trevor, but I didn't." I bite my lip, hoping she buys my story, which technically is true. I really *didn't* see Trevor and since Mom *is* Nessie, that's true, too.

"Darn," she replies, "we don't see her anymore. I'm sorry I missed it."

Diverting her attention, I ask, "What's in the cooler? I'm famished."

Angelina pulls a cold Coke out of the ice and playfully tosses it at me.

I catch it—barely. "Hey! Thanks a lot! Now it will spray all over." Pretending I'm going to open the can pointed at the sand, at the last second, just as I pull the tab, I aim at her, spraying her with exploding stickiness.

She gasps, then laughs. "Okay, I guess I had that coming."

While she washes off the soda in the ocean, Billy and I lay the food out on our towels—sandwiches, dill pickles, and potato chips.

Izzie's on holiday, spending the Fourth of July with her sister in Long Beach. But before she left, she loaded the fridge with food for the celebration tonight. All Dad has to do is barbecue the meat. It'll probably be burned or raw in the middle.

Maybe Marni knows how to cook. That would be a point in her favor.

"Are you going to tell Angelina about your mom?"

Billy's question startles me out of my musings. "I feel bad not telling her. But Mom said not to. I don't know what to do!"

"She'll be hurt if you don't. Do you really think your mom will mind so much?"

I know he's right, but I cringe at the thought. "I want to tell her. Let me think about it. I should ask Mom first."

"Did you find out where she lives?" He sounds as worried as I feel.

"South of here a few miles," I fudge. "But she said I could live with her if I want."Billy visibly cheers up, his eyes crinkling, the corners of his mouth turned up in a satisfied smile. "That's great news!"

I wish I could feel happy, but having to choose between Dad and Mom makes my insides itch.

"Shhh. Here comes Angelina." I try to appear busy foraging in the food bag.

When Angelina returns, shaking water off like a dog, we dive into our feast, laughing and goofing off. The afternoon floats by, filled with Frisbee and body surfing.

At 5:00, we reluctantly leave our umbrella and towels for later, and go to our separate homes, promising to meet up with our parents to watch fireworks.

I bang in the door. Dad steps out of the kitchen wearing Izzie's Kiss-the-Cook apron, a pair of tongs in his hands. Uh-oh. That can't be good. He looks like the Pillsbury Dough Boy.

"Sweetheart! You're home! I just put shrimp on the grill. Are you hungry?"

"Famished!" I respond, hugging him around the waist.

Marni opens the back screen. "Can I help with anything?"

"No, darling, you just relax. Arie and I can do this."

Darling? Ugh. I give him a you've-got-to-be-kidding look. "Dad. Seriously. Let her help."

Marni winks at me. "You'd better let me take those tongs, Jerry." She gently pries them out of Dad's fingers. "You can set the table."

Grudgingly, I admire her ability to size up the problem and come to the rescue. Maybe there's hope here, after all.

During dinner, Marni pesters me with questions about the shops we're going to visit tomorrow, where to buy books (okay, she likes books, that's something, anyway) and where we should have lunch. I chatter on about Laguna Beach Books, Rocky Mountain Chocolate Shop, and Urth Caffe.

The perfect summer day blends into evening, blurring the edges of the sharp shadows as a cool breeze eases the heat.

"It's getting late, ladies. We'd better clean up and get to the beach. There won't be any good spots left." Dad begins to pick up plates, and Marni and I help.

"Billy, Angelina, and I saved a spot!" I chirp. "We just need to get some extra chairs. Billy's mom and dad, and Angelina's mom are coming, too."

"How fun!" Marni responds. "I look forward to meeting all of your friends."

"I'll get the chairs." Rushing to the garage, I brood on Marni's last words. Why does she want to meet everyone only to take us away from them?

We each carry a chair and walk to the cove, Dad also carrying a small cooler, with me in the lead, my bright mood dampened. Determined not to let it get me down, I hurry ahead, focusing on Billy and Angelina and fireworks.

I wish Mom could be with us.

"Look, Dad! There's Billy and Mr. and Mrs. Hernandez." Billy's mom and dad sit in sand chairs, sipping drinks while Billy plays Hacky Sack.

He spots us and jogs over, kicking the Hacky Sack in my direction, which I barely manage to catch with the one hand not holding the chair.

Billy's dad stands up to greet us. "Jerry, it's good to see you."

"Bill, how've you been?" Dad says, shaking Billy's dad's hand. "This is Marni." Dad introduces her, proudly stepping behind her, his hand on her back as if to push her forward.

What is it with her back that he has to keep touching it? Ick. I turn away and ferociously kick the bag back to Billy, who easily balances it on one foot and returns it. Distracted, I miss.

Billy's mom, a tall brunette with an athletic build, rises, and they go through the formalities of more introductions. Billy and I walk down to the water's edge, kicking the bag back and forth along the way.

"What did you do today with your mom?" Billy asks, neatly kicking the bag at me.

As I rush to volley it with my heel, I say, "Mostly messed around at the beach and went swimming." Taking my mind off the game for a second, I spot Angelina and her mom coming down the steps. Billy takes the opportunity to lob the soft bag into my face. I pick it up and sling it at him. He blocks the blow with his elbow.

"Cheater!" he shouts with glee. "No picking up the sack. You lose!"

"Fine, Billy-willy!" I grin. "It's a dumb game, anyway."

"You're only saying that because you lost!" he gloats. He pockets the sack and we stop and wait for Angelina.

Angelina's mom is short like Angelina, delicately thin and pretty. With her blue eyes and buttery blonde hair hanging to the middle of her back, she's a grown-up Angelina but with longer hair. She looks relaxed in faded jeans, a white tank top, and flip-flops, carrying a sand chair and a blue sweatshirt hoodie.

A smile lights up her face.

Angelina introduces her, and Billy's mom welcomes her, clearing a space by moving her chair closer to her husband. The three of them—Mrs. Price, Mrs. Hernandez, and Marni—immediately begin to chatter. Marni pulls out some wine and glasses from the cooler Dad brought, and they get down to the business of being adults.

Angelina, Billy, and I wade in the lapping waves, play Frisbee at the water's edge, and kick the hacky-sack around until the sun goes down with a dramatic display of pink and purple rimmed clouds.

We arrange our towels in front of the adults, readying ourselves for the show. It seems like forever. A big boom startles us, even though we've been expecting it.

Billy scoots closer and takes my hand under the blanket wrapped around the three of us. The fireworks explode to the patriotic songs blaring from Main Beach, working their magic.

As I gaze out at the fireworks reflecting off the water, the finale lights up the surface of the ocean. And there's Mom in her Nessie form, longingly studying the group of us watching from the sand.

Chapter 23

A heavenly scent fills my room. Something's baking. That means Izzie's back! It's not her famous chocolate cake. Cinnamon rolls? No. Muffins? Yes! Blueberry, I hope. Then I hear a laugh—Marni's laugh. She's here already. Disappointed but resigned, I drag myself out of bed. Today is shopping day.

Oh joy. A whole day with Marni. When is she going home, anyway?

Trying to leave my grouchy thoughts in my room, I join Dad, Izzie, and Marni in the kitchen. On the bright side, this might be my big opportunity to win Marni to my side.

"Mornin', Sugar Plum," Izzie says as she expertly removes a tin of blueberry muffins from the oven, flips them onto a plate waiting on the table, and carefully turns them over, top up.

"Glad you're back. Dad managed to not burn the house down while you were gone, thanks to Marni's help," I joke.

Izzie raises an eyebrow.

Izzie knows me better than anyone on the planet, even Billy. She can always tell when I'm faking it.

Dad guffaws and Marni gives me a puzzled half-smile, not sure what to make of the compliment.

I'd better be careful if I want her to like me enough to move here instead of dragging me to Indiana. She's shrewder than I thought. Not like Dad, who falls for it every time.

I guess Izzie decides that at least I'm trying because she hugs me hard, lifting me off the ground. "I missed you," she says, setting me back down.

"I missed you, too!" I'm also relieved. It'll be easier with Izzie here to remind me of my manners.

Dad grabs a pitcher of fresh-squeezed orange juice from the fridge while I get the glasses out of the cupboard and place them next to the plates on the half-set table. Izzie scrapes scrambled eggs from the skillet into a bowl next to the muffins.

"Do you still want to go shopping . . . Marni?" I ask as I rummage in the cutlery drawer for forks.

Izzie gives me a surprised, what-are-you-up-to stare.

"Of course! I wouldn't miss it for the world," she gushes.

I wish she wouldn't try so hard. It makes things worse.

I plunge on. "Great! Angelina will be here at ten. That's when most of the stores open. Where do you want to go first?"

"Is there a bookstore in town?"

Chalk up a point for Marni. She likes books.

"There's Laguna Beach Books. It's my favorite store and near Thalia Surf Shop where you can buy a sweatshirt like mine, though we'll probably want to take the trolley there. It's only about a mile and a half, but mostly uphill." If I have to go shopping, at least I can steer her to the good places. I won't have to pretend. I don't think I can fake it in those boring touristy places.

After breakfast, Marni tries to help clean up, but Izzie won't hear of it, so Dad takes her for a walk on the beach. At last I'm alone with Izzie.

The first thing she says is, "Are you behaving yourself?"

"Well . . . I'm trying. She's not so bad, I guess."

"Just give her a chance. That's all you can do. But always be polite. There's no excuse for rudeness."

"I haven't been rude." My brain, Google-like, races through my mind, pulling out snippets of behavior, some of them not so guilt free. "Mostly, anyway," I confess.

Izzie puts an arm around one shoulder, giving me a little squeeze. "As long as you're doing your best. I know it's tough, trying to let someone new into your life, but I'm proud of you. I don't expect you behave like an angel all the time."

"Good thing because we both know I can't."

"Ain't that the truth, girl!"

It feels good with Izzie here. I can be myself. We finish the kitchen then putter in the garden, pulling bugs off plants and picking vegetables, mostly silent, enjoying the warmth of the sun and each other's company. My mind wanders happily along and then stops on a snag. Harry.

"Izzie, have you seen Harry?" I ask, embarrassed by having completely forgotten about my friend, caught up in my own uncanny soap opera.

"I did. Right before I left for my sister's house. I packed him enough food to tide him over for a couple of days." She jerks out a weed that dared to crop up in her garden.

"What's wrong?" I ask. "Is he okay?"

Izzie stops her foraging, sits back on her knees, and pulls off her gardening gloves. "To tell you the truth, honey, I don't think so. I tried to talk him into seeing a doctor, but he wouldn't budge. I made him take my phone number as an emergency contact and put it in his wallet, just in case. I'll try again today while you're off with Marni. If you see him, text and let me know."

"I will. I'm worried, too. I don't want anything to happen to Harry."

"Don't fret. I'll look after him. You enjoy your day with your dad's lady friend."

"Not much chance of that," I mumble.

Izzie lets me get away with that one. She picks up her basket and heads into the kitchen, while I trail behind.

Angelina arrives, and we sit on the porch, waiting for Dad to come back with Marni.

"I have something to tell you," I whisper. "But I don't want anyone else to hear." I've decided to tell her about Mom, the part Billy knows. I don't think Mom will mind. At least I hope not.

"What?" she whispers back, leaning in for the secret.

"I found my mom."

"WHAT?" She practically jumps off the steps.

I grab her hand, tugging her back down beside me. "Shhhh! Keep quiet or Izzie will come out to investigate."

"Sorry," she says, her voice so small I can barely make out the words.

"My mom's the sand writer."

"I knew it!" she gloats.

I fill her in on the details, keeping an eye on the street and one ear listening for Izzie's footsteps. When I spot Dad and Marni, we stop talking and stand, trying to pretend eagerness to be tour guides.

"Are you girls ready for a day on the town?" Marni asks. She's pretending, too. Her voice has that phony quality adults use when they have to do something they don't particularly want to do but are trying to be polite.

"Sure," Angelina says. "Let's go. Arie says you want to go to the bookstore first. It's really cool."

"Have fun," Dad says, eyeing all of us, but lingering on Marni, his eyes all goofy. He leans over and kisses her on the cheek.

Her eyes go all mushy, too.

Ick. Ick. Ick.

"Lead the way, ladies," Marni links an arm in each of ours, all cozy, like we're best buddies.

I stifle the urge to yank away from her.

She lets go so we can all get through the gate, and then links our arms again. I want to break into hysterical laughter at the thought of us walking down the street this way. It's weird. I hope no one sees us.

When we reach the corner, Marni finally untangles her arms from ours. As we stroll through the streets heading for the trolley stop, Angelina chatters like a monkey, pointing out the Laguna Art Museum, the Starbucks on the corner, surf and scuba shops, Carmelita's restaurant (suggesting that my dad take Marni there), and other places.

After an eternity, the trolley finally pulls up, half empty as it's too early for most of the tourists. Angelina continues her tour-guide babble, saving me from having to make small talk.

We hop off at the Brooks Street stop, and Angelina, now the official tour guide—I so love her right now—leads the way.

"It used to be a pottery store," Angelina informs us, "but it went out of business. It's better as a bookstore, though."

I try to see the shop through Marni's eyes, noticing details I hadn't paid much attention to before. It crowds in among several other shops, a simple, old-fashioned store. Its sign, painted blue with a white wave underlining a palm tree, juts out from the top, hanging like a chandelier over the sidewalk, swaying above the bay windows stacked with books. The store's clay-pink frame accents the sign.

As the bell tinkles when we open the door, Marni exclaims, "How charming!"

Her eyes light her face, her mouth pleased with what she sees.

Hmmm. She really likes it.

"It's not as big as the Barnes and Noble in Aliso Viejo, but we like it," I tell her.

"I can see why. It's marvelous," she says, inhaling like it's a bouquet of roses. "People talk about the 'new car' smell, but I prefer the scent of new books." Her eyes scan the shelves, taking in the bright white walls softened by the creamy-tan bookcases, the carousels filled with flower stencils, the racks of odds and ends, the cushy chairs inviting readers to sit and savor the books.

Knock me over with a feather. I would have sworn she'd prefer the big glitzy bookstores.

Someone who loves books and small bookstores can't be all bad.

Angelina bolts for the children's section while I linger behind with Marni, curious. She trails slowly through the aisles, lovingly running her fingers along the book spines, occasionally pulling one out, reading the jacket, and then carefully placing it back on the shelf. She seems to have forgotten I'm here. I clear my throat to remind her.

"Oh, Arie! I'm sorry. You startled me." A nervous giggle escapes her throat. "Why don't you join Angelina? I'll catch up in a bit." She turns back to the thick book she's chosen, something about Henry VIII, lost in another world.

Surprised at this side of her, I shuttle toward the children's area, occasionally glancing back at Marni, who doesn't notice. Maybe this can work. I need to think up other ways to make her like it here, to like *me.*

Angelina sits cross-legged on the floor, a pile of books beside her, one opened. She's leaning over it, slowly turning the pages. It's not good to disturb her when she's like this, surrounded by books. She'd resent the interruption.

Nothing for me to do but start my own pile. After a few minutes, I've found four promising titles and quietly sit beside Angelina, absorbed in fantasy, trying to decide which one I like best—*Island of the Blue Dolphins, A Wrinkle in Time, Stargirl,* or *The One and Only Ivan.*

Time slows. The sunlight through the windows makes me drowsy. Dust particles glitter in the streams of light. I don't know how much time has passed, but I'm getting stiff from sitting in the same position on the floor, so it must be at least an hour. The soft pad of footsteps on the carpet arouses me, and I look up to find Marni, smiling down at us.

"Have you girls found something you like?"

"Plenty!" Angelina exclaims.

"How about you, Arie?" Marni asks.

"This one looks good." I hold up *The One and Only Ivan,* a story of a gorilla kept in a cage at a mall, told through the eyes of the gorilla.

"May I see it?"

I hand it over and Marni sits down beside me, sets her own book on the floor, and reads the jacket blurb for *Ivan.* "This looks like a beautiful story. I see why you've chosen it. Which one is your favorite, Angelina?" Marni asks, still holding onto my book.

Angelina holds up her prize, *Friday Barnes, Girl Detective.*

No surprise there.

Marni reaches for it, and Angelina hands it over as she glances at me.

"Okay, let's check out and visit the surf shop." Marni stands up, still clutching our books as well as her own.

"But we didn't bring any money," Angelina says.

"It's on me. I'm always happy to buy books for children. I'm just thrilled you both like to read. It opens up so many worlds and experiences." She hugs the books to her chest.

"But . . ." I try to protest.

"No buts. I insist." She walks briskly to the checkout stand, all business, leaving Angelina and me behind.

We put the other books back while Marni chats with the sales lady ringing up our purchases.

"You have to admit, she's pretty nice to buy us books," Angelina says, her voice low so Marni won't overhear.

"Yeah. I suppose so. Or maybe she's just trying to bribe me to like her."

"Who cares? We get new books and it makes her happy."

That's Angelina, all practical.

At Thalia Surf Shop, Marni quickly finds a sweatshirt just like mine only blue. "Don't you girls want to look around?" she asks.

"We can come here any time," I reply. "Besides, Izzie buys most of my stuff online."

"And my mom just bought me a sweatshirt," Angelina adds.

"Okay, then, time for lunch!" She stuffs her new prize into the bag with our books, and we follow her out the door.

At least she's not one of those fussy shoppers who tries on everything in the store before deciding.

We stroll to Urth Caffe and sit at a table outside shaded by a huge green umbrella. Scanning the menu, Marni asks, "What's good here?"

"Everything!" Angelina exclaims.

"Especially the pizzas. Dad and I have tried them all. And he loves their coffee," I add.

"Pizza it is, then. Do you girls have a favorite?"

"Primavera!" we answer at the same time, making us giggle.

Marni orders the pizza, a salad, coffee, and root beers for us.

This day isn't nearly as awful as I thought it would be.

An ambulance screams by, startling us out of our peaceful lunch, sending my heart racing.

"Goodness!" Marni exclaims. "I hope no one's hurt."

"It's probably a tourist caught in a rip-tide having a panic attack. It happens sometimes." I take another bite of pizza.

"Let's hope that's all," Marni mutters.

After lunch, we decide to walk back home on the beach side of the street, stopping at the artist village overlooking the ocean, window shopping and admiring the various displays of handmade pottery, blown glass, paintings, and other items. Marni buys a small, thin hand-blown bud vase and tucks it in with her other purchases.

An hour later, Marni declares she's worn out, so we cross PCH and trudge up the trail to my house.

When we get to the turn, Angelina says, "Sorry, guys, but I told Mom I'd be home early to go shoe shopping." She looks down at her faded flip-flops.

Marni fishes Angelina's book from the bag and hands it to her.

"I'll see you later, Arie. Thanks for the book and lunch, Marni. I had a nice time."

"You're quite welcome, Angelina," Marni replies. "I hope to see you again before I go home."

When we reach the cottage, I stop dead cold. Izzie's sitting on the porch steps, teary-eyed, a cage on her lap holding a small squirrel huddling in a corner.

Chapter 24

My heart sinks to my stomach.

"What happened to Harry?" I rush to Izzie. She puts Penia down and stands to crush me in a hug.

"He had a heart attack, Sugar Plum. I don't know all the details yet. Thankfully, I was with him and called an ambulance. Stubborn old fool. He asked me to bring his squirrel to you to look after, said you'd promised him. I borrowed the cage from a neighbor, afraid the little critter would get scared and run away. I tried to reach you, but you must have your phone on silent."

"I'm sorry, Izzie. I turned it off in the bookstore and forgot to turn it back on. The ambulance went right by us, but I never thought it was Harry!"

Dad pulls into the driveway. "What's happened?" he asks, hurrying out of the car. "Is everyone all right?"

"It's Harry," Izzie explains. "He's in the hospital. It's his heart."

"I'm so sorry, Izzie." Dad's forehead creases in concern. "Is there anything I can do?"

"No but thank you. I'm heading to the hospital now. I only waited for Arie to get home and look after his pet." She lifts the cage, and Dad peers inside.

"A squirrel! How remarkable." Dad studies Penia as she backs away from his giant face, squeaking her irritation.

"Do you think that's safe, Jerry, letting her take care of a squirrel? Rodents carry all kinds of diseases."

Marni. I forgot she was there. Who does she think she is telling Dad what I should or shouldn't do?

I cast my evilest eye at her but she doesn't seem to notice. She's busy studying Dad's reaction.

"You have a point." He runs his fingers through his thinning hair and straightens up. Penia shivers in the corner of her prison.

"Dad! You have to let me take care of her. I promised Harry." I turn to Marni, "And she's not a rodent to me!"

"It's okay, Jerry," Izzie cuts in. "I took the squirrel to a vet a couple of weeks ago, worried it would pass something on to Harry. She's clean. No diseases or parasites."

Good ol' Izzie to the rescue. She never told me about that. I smirk in triumph at Marni. Either nobody notices or they choose to ignore my dramatics. I open the cage and reach in. Penia scampers up my arm and sits on my shoulder, trembling, trying to hide under my hair, her little heart fluttering like hummingbird wings. "It's all right, girl," I soothe. "I'll take care of you." She nuzzles my ear and relaxes a little. "Thank you, Izzie."

Dad looks relieved. "Oh, good. That's very kind of you, Izzie. I'm sure Harry appreciates it."

Marni squints her eyes, still disapproving.

Izzie puts on her sternest expression, aimed right at me. "Arie, the vet issued a special permit for Harry to keep her. You really shouldn't make a pet of a squirrel, but seeing as Harry had already done that, the vet relented. If we returned it to the wild, it probably wouldn't survive. There's an article on your bed for you to read, the proper food and equipment," Izzie lectures. "The vet emailed it to me when I called to tell him what happened and ask what to do."

"I'll take care of her, I promise."

"I know you will. You're a good girl."

I cuddle the tiny squirrel under my chin.

"Now that's settled, I'll get to the hospital. I'm on pins and needles about Harry." Izzie grabs her purse and car keys.

I watch as she buckles in, fires up the engine of her yellow Volkswagen, and pulls away from the curb, leaving me moping on the porch with Dad and Marni, worried for my friend. If not for Harry, I might never have found Mom. I wish I could go with Izzie, but at least I can help by looking after his pet.

I continue my scathing looks at Marni. The day started out so well. Why couldn't she have minded her own business? I was even beginning to like her a little.

"Don't you like animals?" It comes out a little snottier than I'd intended.

Without hesitating, she looks me straight in the eye. "I love animals of all kinds. But wild is wild, and it's often difficult, if not impossible, to completely tame a wild creature."

Dad shifts from one foot to the other, obviously uncomfortable with the conversation. He must be thinking about Mom, the wild creature he couldn't tame.

"Penia's tame enough." I manage to control my tone a little better, but it's still ringed in resentment. "Harry raised her from a baby."

"I'm sure it's all right, Arie. I apologize for interfering. I was worried it would bite you. They can carry rabies and other illnesses."

"Dad doesn't need help worrying about me. He does enough of that by himself," I grumble.

Dad laughs a little nervously. Marni turns away, studying a yellow butterfly flitting around the pink begonias that surround the porch. Izzie planted them to replace the spring daffodils and Irises that 'ran their course,' as she put it. "I'll be in my room reading that article so I'll know what food we need to get. Can you take me to PetSmart after?" I address Dad while Marni pretends to still be fascinated with the butterfly.

"Sure, sweetheart. Just let us know when you're ready."

Us? Does Marni have to be included in *everything* now? "Thanks, Dad." I pick up the cage, and with Penia on my shoulder, walk past Marni without saying a word.

I shut my door a little harder than necessary, place the cage on the dresser, and sit on the bed to read. Penia races around me, full of mischief. I make a list, put Penia in her cage, and find Dad and Marni in the backyard, sipping iced tea.

"I'm ready," I announce.

I'm silent in the back seat on the drive to PetSmart, trying not to brood on the sad turn the day has taken. Dad and Marni chat about anthropology stuff.

I hurry out of the car as soon as it stops, not waiting for them, and rush in. I flag down the first employee I see, a friendly lady with kind blue eyes who leads me around the store, choosing the proper items from my list. Dad and Marni find us in the small pet aisle comparing ferret cages.

"The article says we need a ferret cage she can climb around in. The one she has is too small," I inform Dad, trying to impress him with my attention to the details.

He looks at a price tag and whistles. "That's a steep price for a squirrel cage," he complains to the sales lady.

"Yes, but it's sturdy and roomy. The animal will be happy and won't be able to get out," she replies.

"Okay," he sighs. "Ring us up."

In addition to the cage, we buy the proper balance of food the vet recommended, toys, a nesting box, a water bottle, a leash and harness, and vitamins.

"That's over $300 dollars. That squirrel will be better taken care of than I am," Dad jokes, taking out his credit card and reluctantly handing it over to the sales lady.

When we get home, I hurry to my room and set everything up, exchanging the too-small cage for the new one, cozying the nesting box with paper-thin wood shavings, filling the water bottle and attaching it to the cage, and placing the whole thing back on the dresser. The article says squirrels like to be up high. They feel safer that way.

When I set her in, she explores her new home, her teeny nose twitching with curiosity. She wrestles for a while with a feathery, stuffed toy mouse. I watch her play until she tuckers out and falls asleep, curled up next to her toy in the nesting box. Squirrels mostly sleep in the afternoon but are more active in the mornings and late afternoons, I learned. I tiptoe out, close my bedroom door, tell Dad where I'm going, and head to Billy's.

He's in the garage with Angelina, waxing surfboards. I grab a cloth and help, explaining while we work what happened to Harry and Penia.

"Let's finish up and go to your house to wait for Izzie," Angelina suggests.

"Good idea. We can play with Penia, too. I bet she'd like that," Billy adds.

When we get back, she's still asleep, but Izzie calls to tell us Harry is okay, though he needs a serious operation. He'll be in the hospital for a while, two or more weeks.

"I hope he's going to be all right." I nervously twist a strand of hair.

"Try not to worry, Sugar Plum. Harry says thank you for taking care of his pet. Be a good girl. I won't be around for a few days until I know Harry's out of danger."

"Tell Harry we said hi. I'll take a picture of Penia so you can show him that she's safe."

"That's very thoughtful of you, Arie. I'll be sure and show it to him."

We hang up and I snap a photo of Penia asleep in her nest and text it to Izzie.

"Since Harry's okay, let's go to the beach," Billy suggests.

As if on cue, Penia wakes up and starts chattering for attention.

"We can take her with us. She's used to being outside." I struggle Penia into the harness and leash. At first, she fights to get out of it but eventually calms down.

"Dad!" I yell. He's out back having drinks with Marni. Again. She might as well get a tent and camp out there. "We're going to take Penia for a walk."

"Okay," he shouts back. "Be home in time for supper."

We take turns holding her leash, but she's more determined to climb up our legs than she is to walk. She's a funny little thing, full of spunk.

On the boardwalk, people stare, some stopping to ask questions about Penia, who seems to love the attention. She sits on her hind legs, tsking and chirping away at them. Dogs stop to sniff or bark at her, but she doesn't seem at all afraid, only thumps her foot like a rabbit and flicks her tail. When we get to Fisherman's Cove, it's late afternoon, 4:00, and most of the crowd—at least what passes for a crowd at this slice of beach—have left. We sit on the sand at the edge of the shoreline, filling Billy in on our day with Marni.

"Sounds like it went well." He pulls a bag of peanuts out of his pocket and hands it to Penia. Her tiny claws snatch the prize, and she nibbles fast, as if she's afraid he'll change his mind.

"Do you have any more? I want to try." Angelina reaches over and delicately pets the squirrel.

Billy hands Angelina a peanut. Penia does a little dance in front of Angelina, earning her reward.

"When's Marni going home?" Billy asks.

"Soon, I hope. I don't know how much longer I can take it. She's got no right to tell Dad I shouldn't take care of Harry's squirrel. She's not the boss of me."

"Didn't you say she apologized, though?" Angelina reminds me.

"Yeah, but still, if she's trying to boss me now, what will happen if Dad marries her? She'll think she's my mom."

We fall silent. We're just kids. Adults can make us do whatever they want, and there isn't much we can do about it.

"I wish Nessie would show up." Angelina breeches the silence. "We haven't seen her in a long time. Do you think she's all right?"

"I'm sure she is," I answer, hating myself a little. "We just need to get here at the right time." I chew on the inside of my lip. "Have you seen Trevor?" I ask Billy. I'm getting too good at changing the subject. It makes me sad.

"I forgot to tell you guys. I saw him yesterday. He's going on a cruise with his parents. Somewhere in Europe."

"Wow. Must be nice," Angelina says, sounding wistful and maybe a bit jealous.

"I'd better start home." I stand, brush off the sand, and pick up Penia. "I need to feed her."

After Angelina turns to go home, Billy takes my hand. "Can I come over later?"

"Sure. I'll text you after dinner."

He squeezes my hand and I squeeze back.

When we reach my gate, Billy makes sure no one is looking, and then gives me a quick goodbye kiss. The burn of an unexpected blush stings my cheeks. Billy just smiles and trots off.

"Dad, I'm home," I shout at the backyard.

"Out here, sweetheart. We'd like to talk to you."

Dad's voice sounds so happy, but it's not usually good news when someone says they want to talk to you.

"Okay, I'll be there in a minute. I have to feed Penia." I tuck her in her cage, mix the vitamins into her food, and get fresh water.

Straightening my shoulders, ready to face whatever, I join them, taking a seat next to Dad and away from Marni.

"I hear you have a birthday coming up." Marni folds her hands on the table and leans over like she has some big secret to tell.

I glance at her and then Dad. Uh-oh. This can't be good.

"We're wondering what you'd like to do. Thirteen is a big birthday," Dad adds.

"I don't know. I haven't thought about it." We? What has *she* got to do with my birthday?

"Would you like a party?" Dad asks. "Marni said she'd help you plan it since Izzie is busy with Harry."

Wonderful. That's all I need. What I say is, "No, thank you."

"What do you mean, no, thank you? Every kid likes a party." Dad sounds like he can't believe what he's hearing.

Marni unfolds her hands and studies her fingernails.

"I don't. Besides, the only kids I like are Billy and Angelina." Izzie's image looms large, so I add, "It's very nice of you, Marni. Really. But it's too much trouble for just the three of us. I don't like crowds."

"Okay, honey, you think about it. Maybe you'd all like to go to Disneyland or something like that instead," Dad offers.

Is he kidding me?! Didn't I just say I don't like crowds?! Sheesh. "Dad. Come on. Have you *met me*? Your daughter, who is against all things Disney?"

"Oh. That's right. I forgot." A slight flash of pink creeps from his neck to his face.

He forgot? The old saying "Crazy in Love" sure is true. Emphasis on the crazy. If Billy acted that way, I'd clobber him.

"I just want to hang out with Billy and Angelina. And Harry and Izzie if Harry gets well by then, if that's okay."

"Whatever you want, sweetie." His voice rings with disappointment.

Is he disappointed in me because I don't want his girlfriend throwing me a party? Or disappointed in general?

"Maybe we can barbeque at the beach?" I suggest.

Dad goes a little pale.

Me on the beach on my thirteenth birthday—he's probably worried Mom will show up. I really want to ask him about what he did to Mom, but now is not the time for a fight. I tuck that back into the back of my mind—for now.

Abruptly changing the subject, Dad asks, "Are you hungry? Marni made potato salad, and I thought I'd throw some hot dogs on the grill."

"Sounds great, Dad. And thanks again, Marni, for wanting to help with my birthday. I do appreciate it."

Dad gets up and shuffles over to the grill.

"I'll set the table. Are we eating out here?" I ask.

"That's fine with me." Marni's voice sounds so small I can barely hear her.

I've really blown it. I need to make it right somehow. If she hates me, it won't help my plans to try to stay in Laguna Beach. But I'm still mad. It's hard to be nice when you're mad.

"Want to help me?" I ask her.

She brightens a little. "I'd like that." She follows me into the kitchen and helps gather everything we'll need.

"The potato salad looks really good. What did you put in it?" I ask. Not that I'm interested, but I need to make her feel better.

She answers, her voice more normal now, with a description of the ingredients. "I use Miracle Whip instead of Mayonnaise, yellow mustard, boiled eggs, onion, celery, paprika, and a smidge of sugar—that's the secret ingredient."

"I'll have to write that down. I'm sure Izzie will want the recipe."

"I'll do that and leave it for her," Marni offers. "Do you have a pencil and paper?"

I show her the pad of paper and the matching pen stuck to the fridge with magnets, and she carefully writes out her list and instructions. I think I fixed things with her. She seems less troubled.

Now all I have to do is convince her to move here.

Chapter 25

Billy taps his secret code on the window frame. I pull and push the tabs on the inside of the screen while he tugs from his side. While he squeezes his ever-taller body through the window, a shoe catches on the latch, sending him sprawling awkwardly on the floor.

Bursting into giggles, I sing, "Have a nice trip. See you next fall!" When did I become one of those silly girls who giggles? I guess love makes you do stupid things.

"Very funny," he grunts.

We sit against the bed's backboard, legs stretched out, playing with Penia.

There's a muffled tap-tap-tap at the door, Dad's knock. "Come in, Dad."

He opens the door a crack and sticks in his head. "Hello, Billy. I didn't know you were here. Do you kids want to watch a movie with us?"

Reading Billy's face, I reply, "I don't think so, Dad, but thanks. We're going to play with Penia and write a letter to Harry."

"That's nice of you. Harry will love that. How about some popcorn, then? We're making a batch."

"Cool," Billy replies.

"Thanks, Dad."

After he retreats, I get out some stationery and we start to write a letter, Billy writing while I tell him what to say. Penia curls up in my lap, her fluffy tail spiraling around her.

Dad left the door open a crack, and their muffled voices seep through like a virus. Popcorn smell fills the room with buttery goodness. They must be in the living room now; I can hear them more clearly. I strain a bit to make out the words.

"I just don't think it's a good idea for her to have a boy in her room at her age, even if they've been friends all their lives," Marni says. "At least make them leave the door open. It's just common sense."

"Okay, if you think so," Dad replies. "But I really don't see the harm."

Billy's eyes meet mine, astonished at this exchange. And I'm furious. Cold rage slithers up my spine.

"Uh-oh," Billy whispers, studying my face, "I know that look."

Dad walks in, carrying a bowl of popcorn and two cans of Sprite. "Here you are. And it's not burned," he says, as if he's accomplished some great culinary feat like on those cooking shows.

"Thanks, Dad." My cold voice must alert him to my mood because he doesn't say anything about the door. He simply hands us the treats—but he leaves the door ajar.

When he's gone, I get up and, resisting the impulse to slam it, close the door with a click.

"Who does she think she is, telling *my* dad not to let you in *my* room?" I pace up and down, trying to work out the anger. Wisely, Billy says nothing, just lets me rant. I go on for a few minutes.

When I finally stop and slump down beside him, he asks, "Tantrum over?"

"For now." I grab a pillow and use it as a punching bag.

"Hey! That pillow never did anything to you," Billy says, trying to calm me down by messing around.

It works a little. "Let's go out to the hammock," I suggest.

"Do you think your dad will mind?"

"I don't plan to ask him," I retort, getting up to yank off the window screen.

"Take it easy! You're gonna rip the screen."

"So?" I put Penia's leash on while Billy hauls himself out the window, saying nothing. I hand him the popcorn and soda and follow him, the squirrel nuzzled to my chest.

We settle into the hammock with Penia's leash around my wrist so she can't get away, and munch popcorn, enjoying each other's closeness. Billy puts an arm around me, and I lean against him, taking in the scent of fresh laundry and lemony shampoo. We lie there a while, gently swaying, watching the night sky and the faint shadows the moon casts across the yard. The branches of the old oak trees form a ring of protection around us, leaves slightly rustling in the light breeze.

"This is better." I snuggle a little closer.

"I wish it could always be like this, you and me in the hammock." He shifts his arm to get more comfortable.

"That might get boring." I scratch Penia behind the ears.

"Maybe. But if I have to be bored, there's no one else I'd rather be bored with."

Crossing my arm over his chest, I close my eyes, resting my head on his shoulder. I tilt my head back, and he kisses me, soft and slow.

An hour later, I'm back in my room tucked in bed when Dad checks on me. I pretend to be asleep, and he quietly shuts the door.

***

In the morning, it's just Dad and me. I forgot to set my alarm, so no chance I can sneak out without talking to him.

"Where's Marni?"

"I thought the three of us could go to breakfast together. We can pick her up at the hotel and go to Nick's Cafe. What do you think?"

Trapped. How do I get out of this one? I'm supposed to meet Mom.

"Gee, Dad, that sounds good, but I promised Angelina and Billy we'd hang out." I hope that sounds honest. It's partially true, at least. Half-truths have become as easy as breathing.

Dad doesn't ask many questions. Maybe it should bother me more, this new superpower I've developed, but it doesn't.

"I'm not sure I like the idea of you off by yourself with no one here to supervise." He frowns.

"It's okay, Dad. I'll text you every couple of hours so you know I'm okay. Please?"

He relents. "Okay, but stay out of the ocean. And don't forget to check in."

If he only knew.

"Sure, Dad." I have my fingers crossed behind my back, my bathing suit on under my clothes, and my backpack packed. I've played with Penia, fed her, and cleaned the cage.

Dad goes to shower, and I take off before he can think of reasons to stop me.

Mom's there, sitting in the sand, arms around her knees for warmth, honey-streaked, chestnut hair shining in the early morning beams of light struggling through the clouds. I stop and watch, dazzled as she tucks a long strand behind one ear. She is so beautiful.

Mom.

I lost her once. I can't lose her again. What will she do if I tell her I can't live with her? Will I still be able to see her? Or will she go away for good? If I become a selkie, I'll lose a life I love. I shake my head as if to shake off the thought.

Right now, I just want to be with her.

As I cross the sand, she turns and stands, arms outstretched. "Aurora." The name sounds so musical when she says it. "You're breathtaking, sweetheart."

A little shy at the compliment, I stammer, "Thanks, Mom."

"I thought you weren't coming." She pulls me in for a hug and I hug back.

"Sorry I'm late. I overslept."

"You're here now. That's all that matters. Are you ready?"

Pulling away, I begin peeling off my sweatshirt and step out of my Vans and board shorts. "I'll stash my backpack behind the bushes so you won't have to waste time stowing them."

"Okay," she says, "I'll meet you in the water outside the breakers."

Mystified, I watch as she dives in and disappears.

I swim out beyond the break line, and dog paddle, wondering what Mom is doing. Then the familiar touch of Mom's selkie-self glides around my legs, startling me at first. I flip and dive under as she twists and turns around me. We race along just below the surface, side by side, mother and daughter. It's strange and wonderful, unbelievable and very real.

When we stop and rise to breathe, I glance back at the shore, farther away than I've ever been. Though it should make me nervous being so far out, I feel completely safe. Mom's silent-selkie form of communication radiates joy. When I put my arms around her sleek neck, she does a shallow dive and begins swimming farther out while I hold on, paddling my legs to help propel us along. When she finally stops, I can barely make out the shore. We're in deep water.

Gliding along the surface, I gaze in wonder at more fish than I've ever seen, large schools of blue fin and yellow-tail tuna, some almost as long as me. Rockfish and whitefish, red snapper and sheepshead swim by, unconcerned with us. It feels so natural, so right.

Mom motions for me to follow. We swim a little longer, and then she abruptly stops. Ahead is a spectacular sight, two blue whales heading straight for us. We don't get many of them here, mostly grey whales. We watch as they pull alongside. In awe, I reach out, running my hand along the side of one as it swims peacefully by, its barnacled skin like sandpaper. The other dives deep, then hurtles upward, pulling half its enormous body out of the water. It's not quite a full breach, but it comes down in a thundering crash, radiating a wave that sends us bobbing like corks on the water.

Next to Nessie, it's the most incredible site I've ever seen.

We stay still, admiring them until they're swallowed by the sea.

We've been in the water for about an hour when Mom suddenly shoots in front of me, a sleek torpedo, joy turned to terror.

"Dive down! Now!" Her silent screaming echoes in my brain. "Hide in the kelp."

Taking a deep breath, I dive, swimming underneath the kelp bed, scanning up to see what has Mom so frightened. I watch in horror as the silhouette of a huge shark, maybe a great white, swims along the surface right above us. As the monster prowls, I huddle into a ball as small as I can get, heart racing and body shaking.

"Stay where you are," Mom commands. "I'll come to you when it's safe."

No need to tell me more than once. I'm scared out of my wits. I may never be able to leave this spot.

Mom's out there, in plain sight, about five feet beneath the shark. "Mom! Hide!" But she ignores my silent plea.

Perfectly still, her small form dwarfed by the giant above, she hovers in the water.

Why doesn't she hide? "Please, Mom, please!" I shout.

Slowly it turns and spots her. It heads straight for her, but she holds her position.

When it's almost upon her, I shoot out of my hiding place and head for the shark's underbelly, ramming it with my head, then leap out of the water, twisting my body into an impossible position. The shark, only momentarily stunned, gets its bearings and pursues me, jaws open as it leaps for my twisting form.

"Aurora, no!" Mom screams.

My acrobatics help evade it as I reenter the water, headfirst, and rocket downward, away from Mom.

Not giving up, it swims fast, this way and that, hunting. "Go away, go away!" I silently chant. For several minutes, it continues its quest for a seal meal—or a girl snack. I doubt it's picky. Mom thrashes around, trying to get its attention, but it swishes nearby, zoning in on me. Ducking behind a kelp bed, I manage to get out of its line of sight, though it's no more than a few feet away, tail thrashing, so close I see one black eye staring into mine and its bloodthirsty teeth as it begins to turn toward me.

Mom renews her efforts to get the shark's attention. "Don't move a muscle," she telegraphs the order to me, but I rocket out from the kelp, desperate now to keep it from pursuing Mom.

I telegraph my own order, calling out for help as I swim, zig-zag fashion, trying to evade its horrifying jaws.

Suddenly, something large and fast crashes into the side of the great white, and three more shapes hit it from below, almost flipping it on its side. Dolphins! It worked! They're everywhere, a dozen at least, darting at it, relentless. Mom and I join in, harassing the wolf of the sea.

Finally, it swims away, the dolphins following, chasing it out of their home range.

Running low on air, I shoot for the surface, Mom following. We inhale deep gulps, and I'm trembling uncontrollably, teeth clacking from fear. Now that it's over, I'm fighting hysteria, so I focus on slowing my breathing.

"It's okay, Aurora, you're all right." Mom presses her seal body as close to me as she can, and I grab on tight, still sobbing. "Let's get you home. Hold on."

Without saying a word, I let her swim us to shore. When we reach shallow water, she gives me a final gentle push, and my feet touch sand. Mom jets away.

My legs have turned to Jell-O, but I manage to haul myself out of the water and collapse on the sand, crying now. Luckily, it's early enough that no one is on the beach except a man and his dog on their way up the stairs. Trying to blend in with the sand, I watch until they disappear.

Then Mom's there, human now, climbing down from the rocks, taking me in her arms, trying to soothe me like she did when I was little. Smoothing my hair, she holds me tight. I'm still shaking, though the crying has stopped.

Eventually, I calm down enough to choke out, "Mom, you can't stay there, in the sea. Please come home. *Please!*"

She doesn't answer. I push away from her. "Mom! You have to listen to me. It might have . . . what if . . .?" I shiver with dread, stumbling over the words. "If those dolphins hadn't answered my call…"

Sighing heavily, she replies, calm as can be, "But they did answer. We're all right. You've had a terrible scare, love. And I'm so sorry. I patrolled that area earlier and it wasn't out there." Strands of her hair are beginning to dry, and she impatiently tosses them out of her face. "I hadn't wanted to expose you to that. But, honey, there are sharks on land, too. Humans do terrible things to each other. At least a shark hunts for food, not for sport. Yes, there is danger in the ocean. But there's plenty of danger in the human world, too."

Not knowing what to say, I rest my head on my knees and cry some more. She sits by my side, quiet, her arm around my shoulders.

When I'm all cried out, I raise my head.

"Are you all right now, Aurora?"

Those anxious eyes, the crease above her nose, her lovely face, beg me to understand.

Mustering what courage I can, I reply, "Yes, I think so." But the truth is I'll never be all right again. How can I, knowing what I know? Why hadn't I thought of that before, the danger she could be in?

"That's my brave, strong girl," she says, then frowns. "You are more powerful than I thought, but you should not have tried to save me, Aurora. When I think what could have happened. . .."

"I couldn't just hide and let it *eat* you!" I tug at my hair to keep from shouting.

"I am grateful, but it's my job to make certain it didn't eat *you*."

We sit in silence for a few minutes.

"Mom, can I ask you something?"

"Of course, sweetheart." She's studying me intently.

"How often does that happen? With sharks, I mean."

The question seems to surprise her. She pulls back, eyes open wide.

"That's only the second time I've had to deal with one. It's really a small part of our world. We learn to avoid them at a very young age, and when we do encounter one, we can usually out-maneuver it. Very few selkies are attacked. Usually the beasts sense something about us that's not quite right for a seal. Unfortunately, regular seals have it much worse than we do. I would have taken a different tactic if you hadn't been there, probably dove for cover immediately as I told you to do. I'm just sorry it happened. So very sorry." She covers her face with her hands, massaging her temples with her fingers.

Laughter and the rattle of sand chairs signal the beginning of the beach crowd, and I rise to leave. She rises with me.

"I'd better go. I'm supposed to meet Billy and Angelina at Thalia Beach to surf. Though I don't think I can go in the water again."

Putting one hand on each of my shoulders and bending over slightly, her eyes intent on mine, she says, "Aurora, don't let this incident keep you from enjoying the ocean. Sharks rarely venture into shallow water. You're perfectly safe. Being part selkie, the ocean lives in you like life's blood. It's part of who you are, and always will be."

I can only nod.

She kisses me on the forehead and turns to go, but stops and asks, "When does your dad's lady friend leave?"

"Tomorrow, I think."

"Okay. If I don't see you before, meet me the day after she leaves. You don't have to swim if you aren't ready. But we should talk."

Later, I kick myself for not having asked her what Marni has to do with anything, but I was too upset to think straight.

Chapter 26

At Thalia Beach, Billy and Angelina pester me for not wanting to surf, calling me a scaredy-cat, even though they know that's not true.

Lamely, I defend myself. "I have a stomachache." It's true. Misery has snarled my insides.

"What happened with your mom?" Angelina asks, as we sprawl on beach towels snacking on apples and store-bought cookies, courtesy of Angelina's mom.

"Not much. We hung out for a while at the beach." What can I say? That we almost got eaten by a shark?

Later, we walk to my house to finish the letter to Harry and play with Penia. When I open the cage, she leaps onto my arm, races up, and then launches herself from my shoulder through the air onto the bed.

"Too bad there isn't a squirrel Olympics," Angelina jokes. "She'd win gymnastics gold."

Dad texts to see if I want to go to a boring artsy-fartsy movie with them. Fat chance of that. I write back: *No thanks, Dad. I'm hanging out with Billy and Angelina*

Having the house to ourselves, we make cheese sandwiches, goof off in the backyard, and text pictures of us with Penia to send to Izzie for Harry. We eat cookie dough ice cream while watching a spooky show on Netflix called *Stranger Things*. After this morning, I could write my own episode.

I still can't shake the terror. And I worry for Mom out there with that monster.

When Dad texts to say they're on their way home, I beg Angelina and Billy to stay so I don't have to be alone with Dad and *Marni*. I don't have to twist their arms too hard. They both get permission, so when Dad and Marni arrive, I have reinforcements.

We spend the evening eating delivery veggie pizza and watching TV. At 9:00, Dad insists on driving Angelina and Billy home, so we all pile in Dad's car for the ride. On the way back, it's just Dad, Marni, and me.

It's a quiet ride. When we get back, I say I'm tired and retreat to my room where I play with Penia and read texts from Izzie.

Harry's doing all right, Sugar Plum. He has his operation in a few days. He'll be fine, don't you worry.

I try to sleep, but every time I close my eyes, I see that hulking shape hovering behind my eyelids. I toss and turn, finally drifting off to sleep right before dawn. I awake worrying about Mom. What if that *thing* is still lurking out there?

I shudder and crawl out of bed, rubbing my gritty eyes.

Dad insists I go with him to take Marni to the airport in Santa Ana, a short drive. I'm grateful it's not Los Angeles. That would be an hour of torture. At least she's leaving. My plan to win Marni over didn't work so well, so onto Plan B.

"I enjoyed meeting you, Arie," Marni says as Dad gets her bag out of the trunk.

I stand there on the sidewalk at the drop-off point, uncomfortable, not knowing what to say. Marni faces me like she's expecting a warm and fuzzy hug or something. I pretend to be engrossed in a trail of ants hurrying across the cement and scratch an itch on the side of my leg with my other shoe, wishing she'd be gone already.

"I know I've upset you, but I'd really like for us to be friends." Hesitantly, she holds out her hand.

"That's okay," I mutter, taking her hand and giving it a light squeeze, but refusing to meet her eyes.

"Well . . . goodbye then." She gathers herself, stiffens her back as if in defiance, and turns to Dad. She kisses him quickly on the mouth and takes her bag. He holds her close for a few seconds, and then she walks into the terminal. He watches her go with longing eyes.

She doesn't look back.

I reclaim my spot in the passenger seat. On the way home, Dad asks, "So what do you think? Do you like her?"

Why is he asking *me*? "Does it matter what I think?"

"Of course it does, sweetheart. Why would you believe it wouldn't?" He shifts in his seat, hands tight on the steering wheel, glancing nervously in the rearview mirror.

"I don't know," I grumble in a bratty voice. "Maybe because you never tell me *anything*."

Dad doesn't have a response to that, so we're silent for a while, and then I say, "I don't like her bossing me around."

"What do you mean, bossing you around?" he asks, glancing at me with his brows puckered. "When did she do that?"

Seriously? Adults can be so clueless. "First, she tried to say I shouldn't keep Penia, and then she said Billy shouldn't be in my room. And you let her." I cross my arms and watch out the window at the hawks soaring through the green hills and valleys, hunting for a meal. I turn away when one swoops down in a killing dive. Nature's cruel show.

It reminds me of Mom in the ocean with the shark. I shove down panic by biting my nails.

He's silent for a minute, then says, "I didn't realize you heard Marni's comments about Billy." He stares straight ahead like he's concentrating on driving. "She does have a point. You're growing up, and I still think of you as a little girl, not as a teenager old enough to be interested in boys."

"But Dad! It's *Billy.*"

"I know, sweetheart," he says. "But Marni doesn't know that."

"Exactly. So, you shouldn't let her say what I can or can't do. She's not my *mom.*"

"No, she's not." He sounds so sad that I'm almost sorry.

After several minutes of uncomfortable silence, he says, "I'll talk to her about it. But sweetheart, you could do with a female influence, someone to talk to about things you don't want to discuss with me."

"That's what *Izzie* is for. She told me when I needed a bra, remember? And she took me shopping to get some. If anyone should boss me around, it's *Izzie,* not Marni." And now I have Mom. At least, I hope so.

"You're right." He sighs and adjusts the rearview mirror for the thousandth time. "I'm sorry, Arie. In the future, I'll make it clear to Marni that Izzie is in charge. She was only trying to help. Don't you like her, even a little?"

It seems like all we do lately is apologize to each other.

"Aside from the bossing, I guess she's okay."

"Then you don't mind if she visits again?" His voice is filled with hope.

"I don't mind," I reply, "as long as she doesn't tell me what to do."

"Truce then?" He crooks his little finger for a pinkie swear and holds it out to me.

"Truce." I twine my finger with his and we shake on it. We drive in silence for a while until I think of what I want to say about Mom.

I have to take the plunge before I lose my nerve. In a cold voice, I blurt, "I know you stole Mom's seal skin."

He almost swerves off the road.

"What?! Who told you that?"

"Mom." I say it without emotion, gauging his reaction.

He doesn't say a word, just sits there until we pull into the driveway, and he shuts off the engine. "How long have you known?'

"A few days."

He puts his arms over the steering wheel and rests his head. When he raises it, he wipes away the tears.

"How could you do something so cruel?" I demand.

"I loved her. I didn't force her to come with me, Arie. I would have given it back to her if she hadn't changed her mind and married me. I'm not a monster. Did she say I did?"

"No, she didn't. But that doesn't change the fact you hid her skin from her and let her suffer." I turn away and stare out the window, wondering what Mom is doing right now, if she's safe.

"You're right," he says, resignation in his voice. "I have no defense for what I did."

"If you had really loved her, you wouldn't have done such a terrible thing," I accuse, turning to face him.

"No, you're wrong. I loved her too much, and selfishly."

He looks at me, pain in his eyes, but I'm relentless. "You lied to me, too, Dad. All these years." I shed a few tears of my own. I think I've cried more in these last few days than I have in almost thirteen years. "Now I understand why you don't want me in the ocean."

"I couldn't stand the thought of losing you, too," he says.

I don't respond, only turn away, to stare out the window at nothing.

"Are you going with her?" he asks.

"I don't know yet." I bite my nails again, though there is nothing left to bite. I almost threaten him with Indiana, but I'm holding that card, giving him another chance to not make me move. Blackmailing, I'm finding out, has its uses.

"Arie, please try to understand, sweetheart," he pleads. "What I've done is wrong, but I thought I was doing it for the right reasons. I hope you can forgive me."

I ignore this last comment because I don't know if I can forgive him, or Mom, either. Instead, I say, "It's getting hot in the car. Let's just go in the house. I need to take care of Penia."

* * *

We've called a silent truce for now and eat leftover pizza for dinner in front of the TV, both of us falling asleep. When I wake up, I turn off the TV, throw a blanket over Dad, and burrow down in my bed. Shadows of sharks still haunt me, but I finally fall back to sleep while reading, keeping my light on in case I wake in the night.

Whispered voices seep into my sluggish brain. It's 1:00 AM. Maybe I'm dreaming. Straining to hear, I sit up in bed. Definitely voices. I tiptoe to the door, listening intently.

It's no dream.

It's Mom's voice, insistent but soft as powdered sugar. "Jerry, we've been over this. Aurora has the right to make up her own mind. You can't take her from here if she doesn't want to leave, no more than you can deny her the right to choose her own path."

"I can't lose Arie." Dad sounds . . . tired? Afraid? Angry? Maybe all three.

I tiptoe closer and peek around the corner. Mom reaches across the table and places her hand over Dad's. "I know it's difficult, but it's wrong to deny her the opportunity to find out who she is. You shouldn't have lied to her."

Dad slides his hand from under hers and rubs the back of his neck.

She's right. He shouldn't have lied to me.

"And you shouldn't have approached her without seeing me first, Kalysta," he retorts. "You're gone for eight years and then just show up out of nowhere?"

"And what would you have done? Run off to Indiana with her?" Mom's voice has a hardness to it, as if straining not to break into jagged fragments like peanut brittle.

"And why shouldn't I? You left us, left her." He massages his temples, his voice angry yet fragile. "I'm the one who stayed and raised her."

"That's not fair, Jerry," Mom accuses. "You know why I had to leave. You refused to see the truth. I was wasting away here. I need the ocean like humans need air."

Dad covers his face with his hands, resting his elbows on the table for support. Mom crosses her arms in defiance. They sit quiet, neither budging.

When he raises his head, his face is wet. "Please don't take her from me."

These two are too much. I stomp into the room. "This is *my* life you're talking about! Don't I get a say in any of this?"

"You're right, sweetheart," Dad says, sounding like he's aged twenty years. "Sit down, we'll all talk."

"I'll make us some tea." Mom goes straight to the cabinet and brings out the tea kettle and chamomile, as if she'd never left, briskly filling it with water and putting it on the stove.

No one says anything. We just wait.

When the kettle whistles, Mom pours the water into the teapot and brings it to the table, along with cups and a bottle of honey. Mom pours, and we mix in honey, stalling the need to talk by blowing in our cups and carefully sipping.

"Your mom tells me she's filled you in on her world. I should have told you a long time ago." Dad takes another sip of tea, tears still pooling in his eyes. "Yes, part of it was selfishness, but I also didn't know how. I didn't think you would believe me."

He sounds worn out. And he's probably right. It's still hard to believe, even with the proof right in front of me.

"Can you ever forgive us?" Mom asks.

"I don't know. I'm mad at both of you, Dad for lying and you for leaving." I focus on blowing on my tea.

"You must have questions," Mom says. "Now would be a good time to ask them."

The moment is right, so I ask Dad, "Are you still going to make me move to Indiana?".

"You don't get to blackmail me. I have the right to be happy, Arie." Dark circles form half-moons under his eyes.

"So Marni is more important than me?" I put my cup down hard, sloshing some of it onto the table.

"That's unfair, Arie," he responds.

"I don't care if it's unfair! You've both been unfair to me."

"Don't use that tone with me," he says.

"What tone? Angry? Hurt? I've a right to be as happy as you!" I cry.

"Your dad is right, Aurora. Calm down," Mom adds.

"Calm down? You've no right to tell me anything!" I shout. "You left me instead of trying to figure out how you could at least stay in my life. You're both cowards!"

They fall silent, Mom's expression shocked, Dad's betrayed.

"I deserve that," Mom says, her voice soft. "I'd better go. Let me know what you decide." Slowly, she stands and pushes in her chair.

Focusing on my tea, blowing on it in quick bursts, I turn to Mom. "If I don't become a selkie, will I ever see you again?" That inner ache poises to clutch at me again, waiting for her answer.

"Of course you'll see me," she says, sounding astonished at the question. "My selkie family and I only migrate as far north as Monterey to colder waters in the summer and come back in the fall. We'll have a late start this year. We stayed this summer for your thirteenth birthday. We'll leave right after that but return in November."

Selkie family? I start to ask her about that, but it's too much to absorb right now. That makes sense, though, the migration. In the past two years, I saw Nessie mostly in fall and winter. The icy ache dissolves, leaving warmth in its wake.

"You don't have to decide now. Wait until your birthday and tell us then. That's the appropriate time, even if you've already made up your mind," Mom says, her voice wistful.

"I haven't," I say, with a toss of my hair.

Her dark eyes search my mind, her longing a shroud on my heart. My spirit feels bruised. How can I make that decision? If I don't go with her, I'll miss part of who I am. I nod, unable to find something to say.

Dad, breaking the spell, says, "Let's not quarrel any longer. It's late, we're all tired and our nerves frazzled. We could use some sleep."

"Aurora, I will see you on your birthday. By then, you'll have to decide."

She turns to leave, but I can't bear to see her walk out that door. "Can you stay here tonight? You can sleep in my room."

She hesitates, glancing at Dad, and replies, "Are you sure you want me to?"

I nod, and she says, "If it's all right with your dad."

"Of course. You're welcome anytime, Kalysta. I'll leave you two alone to get settled." Shoulders slumped, he gives me a quick kiss on the head and goes to his room, closing the door behind him.

I find extra pillows, and Mom and I snuggle under the covers.

"Don't worry, Aurora. It will all work itself out."

"Thanks, Mom." I fall into a dream-free sleep, her arm around me.

Chapter 27

When I awake, she's gone. Did I only dream last night happened? But the pillow next to me has an imprint from her head, and a single strand of her long, dark hair spirals across the white of the pillowcase. Her salty scent lingers in the room. Twirling the hair around my finger into a tight circle, I reach under the bed for my shell-covered treasure box to slip it inside. That's when I notice it, a note in her now familiar handwriting beckoning from the corner of the mirror, stuck between the glass and the frame.

> I'll see you soon. Talk to your dad about what you'd like to do for your birthday.
>
> Love,
> Mom

I pluck the note from its spot, fold it into a tiny square, slip the strand of hair inside like a letter in an envelope, and tuck it into the box and back under my bed.

Dad's clunking around in the kitchen, probably making coffee. I feed Penia and turn her loose in my room to play.

"Hi, Dad." My voice sounds chirpier than it has in a long time. I *feel* chirpier.

"Good morning, sweetheart." He looks a little better this morning but still pale and tired. "Sorry if I woke you."

"No problem, Dad. Can I help?"

"You can get out the cereal."

I pop bread in the toaster and find the box of Raisin Bran.

"Okay, Arie, you win. I talked to Marni this morning. We'll work something out. You don't have to move to Indiana, if that makes your decision less difficult."

I rush to hug him. "Thanks, Dad."

He hugs me close and kisses the top of my head, like he always does. We go on as if nothing has happened, like our world hasn't been turned upside down.

Dad finishes the coffee and, like Izzie, sits at the table with *The Los Angeles Times* open to the crossword puzzle. He's smart in that bookish way of his. On Sunday, he gets *The New York Times* because the crossword puzzle is harder. He likes the challenge.

"I know what I want for my birthday."

He looks up from his bowl with a limp smile, the kind that doesn't quite reach the eyes. "What would that be?"

"A beach barbeque with Angelina, Billy, Izzie, Harry, if he's out of the hospital, you, and Mom."

His Adam's apple moves like he's having trouble swallowing. "I think that can be arranged. Just let me know what you need."

"Thanks, Dad. I'll make a list after breakfast." I hug him on my way to the sink.

***

Three weeks later, Dad drives Billy, Angelina, and me to Fisherman's Cove to unload the party gear. We're crammed in among Tiki torches, a portable grill, lawn chairs, a collapsible table, balloons, and an ice chest filled with soft drinks and hot dogs. Trader Joe's reusable bags overflow with chips and salsa, guacamole, ingredients for s'mores, napkins, paper plates, and Dad's barbeque equipment. It takes several trips to get it all down to the sand.

While we're setting up, Izzie arrives without Harry, who pulled through his operation just fine but is not yet well enough to attend my party. She lugs a bakery box containing my birthday cake, chocolate fudge with maple cinnamon frosting—my favorite.

I'm so happy to see her that I stand there grinning like an idiot. I haven't seen her since Harry got sick.

"That table won't set itself up, girl. Get a move on. This cake's heavy," she says.

I hug her instead, making her laugh.

"Shoo, now, Sugar Plum, and get to work."

Angelina and I set up the table while Dad and Billy dig holes and pound in the torches.

After Izzie unloads the cake, she sprawls in a chair.

"How's Harry?" I ask as I arrange a stack of paper plates on the table, buffet style.

"He's doing fine. He said for you to save him a piece of cake." She shifts in her chair.

"Can we visit him?" Billy wants to know.

"The last thing he needs is a bunch of rowdy kids destroying his peace of mind," Izzie sniffs, her way of telling us the subject's closed. "I'll take it to him tomorrow. He'll be out soon. You kids can visit then."

"Where's he going to stay?" Angelina asks, with a worried frown.

"He'll stay at my place until we figure something out," Izzie says. "He can't stay on the street anymore, that's clear."

I nod, glad Harry has Izzie. I'm glad *I* have Izzie.

"I hear you've been holding out on me, Sugar Plum." Izzie wags a chastising finger at me.

"Huh?" What *is* she talking about?

"Your mom came to see me. We had a nice long chat."

I wonder if Mom told her *everything.* "Sorry, Izzie. I promised I wouldn't tell."

"No need to apologize, girl. I'm pulling your leg. She's back and that's a good thing. I've missed her."

"Me too." All these missing pieces of my life have finally fallen into place like a difficult puzzle.

The sun hangs low in the sky. Dad lights the torches, and then, like a sea goddess, she appears over the rocks, carrying a delicate headband of violets and white daisies strung with tiny pink spiral shells, trailing braided purple ribbons. We all watch, transfixed, as she makes her way to us.

Mom reaches me and fits the garland on my head like a crown, fussing until it's just so. She caresses my face, and I place my hand over hers, enjoying her touch.

"It's beautiful, Mom. Thank you."

"In ancient times, girls wore flower garlands when they turned thirteen, signaling the transition from child to adult. I'm glad you like it. It seemed appropriate." She brushes a lock of hair from my face, tucking it behind my ear and winks.

Though she can't say so, I know she means selkie girls.

"Who wants hot dogs?" Dad asks, a little too loud.

A chorus of "Me, me!" answers him, and he begins setting up the portable grill. Izzie brings out a bottle of pink wine from the cooler and pours some for herself and Mom. Dad opens a bottle of dark brown, stinky beer, and the rest of us pop open cans of frosty Dr. Pepper. We line up the chairs facing the beach while hot dogs sizzle on the grill behind us.

I notice Mom barely sips the wine. Maybe it's because she's a selkie. I doubt they like wine.

When the sun begins to set, Dad holds up his beer and cries, "To Arie, our birthday girl!"

Everyone calls out "Cheers!" as we clink our drinks.

Mom and Dad both here on my birthday—I can hardly believe it's happening.

Dad gets out his camera and makes us all pose for him before the light completely disappears: Mom and me, Izzie and Mom and me, Billy and me, Angelina and me, Billy and Angelina and me. Izzie takes a picture of Mom, Dad, and me—another treasure for my box. Then we all goof around, showing off for the camera, as Dad snaps away.

Izzie makes sure Dad doesn't burn the hot dogs, and we load our plates, eating, talking, and laughing. Mom and Dad seem less tense with each other, though Dad's laughs don't sound quite right, and his sentences often end in a high-pitched squeak. Occasionally, he nervously runs his fingers through his hair while Mom relaxes in a sand chair, regal as a Siamese cat.

"Time for s'mores!" Dad pulls out the portable wood-burning pit, the kind people buy for camping, and gets the fire going. We're not supposed to have fires on the beach, but Dad says no one checks these small coves, only Main Beach and Heisler Park.

I'm surprised. He's usually pretty strict about laws.

We roast marshmallows on long metal skewers until they're almost burnt and stick them between the graham crackers and chocolate bars, so hot the chocolate melts into a gooey, yummy mess.

It's the perfect birthday. I wish it could always be like this.

Mom and Izzie help Dad clear the table, and we play monopoly by torchlight. Angelina shows ruthlessness I would never have suspected, beating us all.

"Forget being a detective. You'll make a great business tycoon," I tell her. Everyone laughs.

"Time for cake," Izzie announces, "though lord knows you all don't need more sugar."

She sticks thirteen candles in and lights them, and they embarrass me with the "Happy Birthday" song. After we finish eating ourselves into sugar comas, Izzie hands me a box about a foot square, and heavy, wrapped in purple and white swirled paper with a glistening purple bow. I can't imagine what it could be. Everyone scoots their chairs in a circle around me.

I take my time, untying the ribbon, carefully removing the tape at the ends, and unfolding the paper.

"Come on, already," Billy complains, "it'll be midnight before you get that open."

I stick my tongue out at him. When I finally pry open the box, a piece of foam bars the way. It takes another couple of minutes to get the casing out of the box and the tape off the two halves of foam. Carefully, I lift it out. Staring back at me is a magnificent porcelain seal, with the exact gold-brown coat as Nessie. It perches on the rocks, gazing out at the sea, bringing tears to my eyes.

"Oh, Izzie, it's beautiful." I hug her. "I'll treasure it always."

"You're welcome, Sugar Plum."

Mom and I share a secretive glance.

"I have something else for you." Mom smiles, reaching into the pocket of her dress and handing me a beautiful white, three-pronged comb, the kind that holds hair in place. Three light blue stones stud the handle and sparkle in the firelight.

"Oh, Mom!" I finger the stones and look up at her. "It's perfect. I've never seen this type of stone. What is it?"

"Aquamarines from the sea." She reaches for the comb and I hand it over. "Let me help you." She rises and kneels behind me, carefully removing the garland. As she expertly twists my hair into a loose bun, she says, "The comb is carved from whale bone found on the ocean floor."

She sits back down and admires her work.

"Wow! That's so pretty," Angelina gushes. "It makes you look more grown-up."

"I assure you that is not my intent," Mom laughs.

Overwhelmed with happiness, I reach over and hug her tight.

After everyone admires my new do, Angelina says, "Open mine next," and hands me a small box.

I open it with less difficulty. Nestled into a slot in the velvet is a silver friendship ring, a Claddagh, like the clasp on my necklace, holding a brilliant green peridot gem, my birthstone.

Angelina holds up her hand to show me its twin except for its topaz stone for November. "Best friends forever."

I slip it onto my finger, a perfect fit. "Best friends forever," I repeat. "I love it, Angelina. Thank you. I'll never take it off."

"You better not," she replies.

"I could never find a better best friend than you," I say.

"Very true." Her eyes twinkle with mischief.

"My turn," Billy says, handing me a box a little bigger than Angelina's.

It's clumsily wrapped, and I love him even more for doing it himself. Inside, a silver rope bracelet glitters in the torchlight, strung with a single, small abalone pearl, matching my necklace. Everyone grows quiet as I hold it up for them to admire. "Help me put it on." I hand it back to Billy. He bends over my wrist and hooks it. Impulsively, I hug him around the neck, whispering, "Thank you. It's wonderful."

Then I notice the adults watching us with too much interest: Izzie and her knowing smile, Mom thoughtful, beaming love and a little bit of suspicion. Abruptly, I sit back in the lawn chair.

I guess another secret is out.

Dad's eyes narrow, his face knotted into an odd, concerned expression, but then he shrugs ever-so-lightly and comes to the rescue. "Now for my gift." He walks over to the rocks and reaches behind, pulling out an awkwardly shaped present, taller than me, wrapped in the same paper as Izzie's gift, overwhelmed with a gigantic silver bow, the kind you see on fancy cars in commercials at Christmas time.

It takes a few seconds to sink in. "Dad? How . . .."

"Your mom told me," he says, simple as that. "Come on, open it!"

"Thank you, Mom!" I call to her. Then I run to him and hug him tight, feeling like I'm in a dream. He holds it while I tear off the paper and bow. A bold Hawaiian print, purple hibiscus flowers with green leaves on a dark background, reveals itself. I run my hands lovingly down its side. My own surfboard.

Good thing I'm getting over my fear of sharks. I can't say it doesn't make me nervous, but I'm working on it.

"Oh, Dad," I say in awe, "I don't know what to say. It's amazing." Everyone crowds around to admire my new board. "I can't wait to try it out. This has been the best birthday ever. Thank you."

He leans in close. "No more secrets, okay?"

"Okay." I don't think I've ever been happier than this very minute.

Angelina, Billy, and I take turns standing on the board in the sand, pretending to ride the waves. We make plans to go surfing tomorrow.

The torches begin to die down, and it's time to go. We pack up and begin hauling everything up the stairs.

Mom pulls me aside. "Can I talk to you a minute?"

"Sure, Mom." She leads me to the water's edge, away from big ears. We stand arm in arm like the first time I met her here and gaze out at the moonlit sea.

"So, you've decided to stay here?" She sounds a little sad but not surprised.

"How did you know?" That's a dumb question.

She simply smiles and brushes my hair out of my eyes. "You have a wonderful life here, Aurora, and you've made the right choice, as hard as it is for me to say. I love you, sweetheart, and it's difficult to say goodbye so soon after I've gotten to know you again. But you're happy and well cared for. Your dad loves you more than life."

"I'll miss you, Mom." She holds me in her arms as I cry a little. I notice she's crying, too.

"And I'll miss you, darling girl. But I'll return soon. Go now. Your father's waiting for you."

I turn to look, and there's Dad, standing at the bottom of the stairs, watching.

I hear a splash behind me, and she's gone.

Chapter 28

Sitting in the sand, watching the changes in the dawn sky as the sun crests behind me turning the clouds various shades of blue and purple and grey, I wait for my beautiful seal, fingering the pearls Mom gave me. It's been over a year since my thirteenth birthday. Mom returned, as promised, last November and stayed until late spring. She swam with me as Nessie, and as Kalysta, she had picnics on the beach with Billy, Angelina, Izzie, me, and sometimes Dad.

She even met Marni. They got along well, and Marni made supper for all of us, vegetarian lasagna, good but not as good as Izzie's.

Marni promised not to boss me, so things have been better with her. She's nice and gives me advice if I ask but keeps her word (though sometimes I think she must bite her tongue). We even have a few secrets we keep from Dad, like boy stuff.

Dad's pleas to Marni to move here finally worked and they got married on Valentine's Day. She transferred to Dad's university and moved here shortly before the wedding. It was a small affair with a few close friends of hers from Indiana and Dad's from the university. And of course, Angelina, Billy, their parents, Izzie, and I attended. Angelina and I wore pink bridesmaids' dresses, dripping with lace—ick. The ceremony took place under the gazebo overlooking the ocean. Billy looked cute in his suit, honored to be best man, his dad a groomsman. Even Harry attended, clean-shaven, smelling of soap, and wearing a suit Izzie got at a thrift store.

Dad has lost the sad expression he always wore. For that reason alone, I can love Marni.

Izzie told me last year I was too old for a nanny. She's right, though it took some getting used to, not having her around all the time. But I still see her several times a week. She opened a bakery/café in town, and it's always packed. Billy, Angelina, and I stop by sometimes after school. Izzie gives us treats, and if it's not too busy, she'll take a break and chat with us or we help her in the back, rolling dough and preparing frosting. If Harry's not around, we do dishes and sweep up.

Harry recovered and took possession of Penia. Izzie fixed up a little apartment above the store for him with a bed, a dresser, and a tiny bathroom. He's much cleaner these days. Harry will never win any personal hygiene awards, but at least the smell doesn't burn out people's nose hairs. He refuses to live there for free, he has his pride, Izzie says, so he helps with the janitor work to earn his keep. Sometimes living indoors gets to him, so he'll disappear for a night or two, sleeping out under the stars. But he always comes back. His doctor put him on new medication for the schizophrenia that agrees with him, so he acts normal most of the time, and Izzie monitors it and his cholesterol pills.

Billy, Angelina, and I whizzed through seventh grade and started eighth this fall. Angelina has a boyfriend now, Ethan, who adores her. We're teaching him to surf. Angelina still wants to be a detective. Sometimes she annoys people because she's always snooping. She writes articles for the school newspaper. Angelina's the best reporter they've got. She says if she can't be a detective, she'll have journalism to fall back on.

Billy won last year's local surfing competition for his age group, and he's had a few offers from surf companies wanting to sponsor him. His dad's handling it all. I told Billy his head would get so big he wouldn't be able to keep his balance on the board.

The eighth-grade swim coach wants me to be on the swim team, but I have no interest in that. I swim faster and farther than anyone else in the school, but the chlorine and the noise of the audience yelling, make me nervous. Though I'm still wary of the sharks, I've not seen another one since that day, but I stick close to the shoreline just in case.

Last summer, I started volunteering at the marine mammal rescue center, helping with the seals and sea lions that get sick or injured, just like Mom used to do. I clean up, mix food, and keep them company. They like to follow me around while I work. The other employees call me the seal whisperer. I tell them I get it from my mom.

At the end of seventh grade, I won an award for the school's writing competition for a short story with an enchanted squirrel as the main character. Mr. Miner, my English teacher, said I should make it into a novel, so maybe I'll do that. I considered writing a story about selkies, but it might raise some eyebrows with Angelina and Billy. I never told them the entire truth about Mom. She thinks it could endanger the selkies if anyone found out.

Occasionally, we still see Trevor at the beach. He's getting tall and awkward but still adorable (and still in love with Reese).

I can't complain. Life turned out pretty good for me. I've let go of the dream of Mom and Dad being together like when I was little. That's a child's fantasy, and I'm no longer a child. I miss her, of course, but I understand. Some things just are, and you have to accept them.

So I wait for her, alone. The ocean's lure is strong, and while I'll never be a true selkie, I'm content to have Mom's way with animals, her love of the sea, and a little bit of her wild nature.

A flicker in the water alerts me, and there she is, her golden-brown head emerging like the first time I saw her.

And by Mom's side, a tiny brown seal pup gazes back at me.

The End

www.ingramcontent.com/pod-product-compliance
Lightning Source LLC
Chambersburg PA
CBHW061256120726
48001CB00001B/326